Tales from the Urals

Of The Lady

and

the Stone Masters

collected and transcribed by **Pavel Bazhov**

translated and co-authored by **Victoria Fé**

Copyright © 2025 Victoria Fé
All rights reserved.
ISBN: 9798345147689

Tales

From the Urals

Letter to the Reader	1
The Stone Flower	4
The Stone Master	32
The Lady of the Copper Mountain	49
The Malachite Box	61
Two Little Lizards	91
The Malachite Necklace	113
About the Authors	132

To Mary,

Thank you so much for attending my reading! Enjoy the book :)

Victoria

Letter to the Reader

Dear Reader,

I thought you deserved a bit of background before you started reading the tales in this book. To begin with, these are not my stories; they are translations of folk tales collected by a Russian writer and publicist Pavel Bazhov — except the last one, which was inspired by the myths and characters you will get to know soon.

If you search Bazhov's works on Wikipedia, you will see a section claiming that those Urals' tales are untranslatable due to cultural and linguistic difficulties. Hence, please forgive me if some parts of what you will read may seem odd. I will also welcome your comments and feedback since I am planning to start a podcast aimed at discussing what is actually going on in these tales.

My professional career as a linguist began with a dissertation on myths and mythology in literature. In addition to that, I have done quite a bit of writing of my own, both fiction and non-fiction. Thus, it is not surprising that, after a long and winding road in the fields of literature, language and philosophy, I have come full circle in an attempt to translate "the untranslatable". My goal here is to make this half-forgotten piece of Russian culture and collective consciousness available to wider audiences.

Not many outside Russia know that, despite its conversion to Christianity over a thousand years ago, Russians have managed to keep a significant amount of their pagan beliefs. The Russian mind has somehow blended their faith in the one-and-only-god with believing in the existence of house, river and forest spirits, and a bunch of superstitions, to boot. Even educated contemporary Russians will knock on wood if they are worried about jinxing some positive future event in the making. I still remember how my grandmother, having moved to a new place, told me she needed to make friends with the new home spirit (called "Domovoy") so he would not cause her any trouble.

Having read the above, you will probably be less surprised to hear about some mythical creatures helping in or hindering people's endeavors in XIXth-century Russia. The tales that you are about to delve into can be best described as magic realism. They blend descriptions of unfair living and working conditions Russian common folks had to endure and a naive belief in some unseen forces who may punish the punishers — if they are so inclined. There is a plethora of magic beings that inhabit the Ural mountains, according to those myths, but this series of stories focuses on the most prominent one — the Lady of the Copper Mountain.

The tales are set in the Urals, the oldest mountain range in the continent which serves as the natural boundary between Europe and Asia. The mountains have long been famous for their rich deposits of ore and a wide variety of minerals — some of which are used to decorate facades of buildings and their interior (like marble and granite). Others, more rare (like malachite or amethyst), are highly valued in the jewelry business and the world of art due to their unique coloring and intricate patterns. The main characters of the tales are villagers who, at that time (1800s), still belonged to the landowner (a Russian barin). Their lives revolved around mining and stone carving. The narrator is one of the village folks, and Bazhov did his best to preserve the simplicity and peculiarity of this person's storytelling manner. I have also tried to keep the spirit of those old tales — that are supposed to sound a bit rough like unpolished stone and common folks they tell us about.

The translation process was no easy feat. On the one hand, Pavel Bazhov resorted to transcribing rather than re-writing the stories, which led him to keeping the broken oral grammar structures and verbs time-traveling from the present to the past and back every other sentence or so — oh, and hardly any punctuation to speak of. On the other hand, the original narration is speckled with regional and time-specific words, which had to be translated into contemporary Russian first — to see how to better relay them in English. I had to make hard choices about which concepts and structures should stay, and which ones should go to avoid overcomplicating the telling of the story.

There are five translated tales in this collection: The Stone Flower, The Stone Master, The Lady of the Copper Mountain, The Malachite Box, and Two Little Lizards. The last story in this collection is my own creation. You might wonder why I added my own story to the bunch, and here is the explanation. By the end of the series all our characters are accounted for, except the heroine of The Malachite Box. I got curious about what happened to her. Hence, there came a sequel called The Malachite Necklace — which, hopefully, won't disappoint you, my reader.

Yours,

Victoria Fé

The Stone Flower

And you know what I'll tell you? The marble masters were not the only ones skilled enough to work with stone. Our guys had a knack for it too. But the difference is which stone, you see. Ours worked with malachite more because there was plenty and it was the very finest kind. And they used that malachite to make things out of. And such marvelous things you see that you'd look and wonder where those designs came from.

So there was this stone master Prokopich. He was first and best in that stone-carving craft. And old he was, so the barin ordered his bailiff[1] to find some youngsters so they would learn from Prokopich.

"Find a good pupil to study the old guy's craft in every detail," he said.

But Prokopich — who knows why, maybe he was unwilling to share or whatever — was the worst teacher, you see. He would show things by fits and starts, and was quick to use his fist. And so he would slap the boy around for a while and pull his ears till they were all red and swollen, and then say to the bailiff "This one won't do… His eye is not sharp enough, and his hand is not steady. Can't make anything out of him."

The bailiff, mayhap, had been told to humor Prokopich. "This won't do, we'll find another one," and he'd bring him another boy, you know.

And so the village lads heard about this and would howl, scream and hide away wherever possible — not to be taken as Prokopich's apprentice. Also, their mothers and

---

[1] A bailiff (outdated) was a hired administrator who managed finances and real estate for the nobles in Russia called "barins".

fathers did not wish to let one of their own be harrowed like that — so they would back out as much as they could. And this trade, you know, is not healthy, to boot. Pure poison it is, is it? Naturally, people would want to stay away.

But the bailiff still remembered the barin's order and looked high and low for new apprentice lads. Prokopich, though, treated each new one in his usual manner and sent him back all the same. "This won't do either..."

The bailiff got hot under the collar, in the end. "This one won't do; that one won't either... How long are you going to keep it up, eh? Teach this boy!"

But Prokopich stuck to his words. "What can I do? Ten years will pass and this boy won't learn the trade."

"So what boy do you want?"

"I don't care, eh? New boy or no boy, same difference..."

The bailiff and Prokopich tried a bunch of youngsters like that, but, in the end, nothing came out of it but slaps and swollen ears and only one thought in the lads' head — how to sneak away. Some spoiled stone on purpose so Prokopich would send them back.

Finally, there was this small boy left, Skinny Danilko. He was an orphan, that one. He was maybe twelve years old or more, and tall, but all skin and bones, so thin. His face was clear, and good-looking he was, curls in his fair hair and bright blue eyes. So they took him on as a houseboy at first, to fetch trifles like a snuff box or handkerchief or to run with a message and such. But he wasn't apt, that one. Other boys would fawn about to please the barin's family. And this one would just hide in a dark corner and stare at a picture or some ornament. He wouldn't even hear when called. They beat him at first, but then gave up on him "Feeble, that one! So slow, won't make a good servant out of him."

Yet, they didn't send him to the plant or the mountain either — so skinny he was he wouldn't last a week. Instead, the bailiff made him a shepherd's help. But even there Danilko was no good. And it was not for the lack of trying. He did try, but still he could not do a good job. It's like he was always up in the clouds thinking about something. The shepherd would catch him staring at a blade of grass — and the cows are far ahead already!

The old shepherd was kindly, though, took pity on the orphan but still got mad at him at times. "What will become of you, Danilko? You'll do yourself in, will you? And my old back, too, will suffer. What are you good for? And what is it you think about?"

"I don't reckon really, grandpa. Nothing much... Just looking maybe. So there was this little bug on that leaf. And the bug is dark-blue, it seems like, but underneath its wings something yellow shows, and the leaf is green and wide. And its edges are pointy and curved, here dark-green, but the middle of it is bright — like freshly painted. And the bug just crawls along."

"Such a fool you are, Danilko. What's your business looking at bugs? Let it crawl, your task is to look after the cows, ain't it? Stop fooling around, will ya? Or I'll tell the bailiff!"

One thing Danilo got good at, you know. When he learned to play the oat[2], no one could match him! Such music it was. In the evening, when they brought the cows back from the meadow, all the girls and women would plead "Play us something, Danilushko, will you?"

And he would play. And the tunes are all unfamiliar, odd ones. Like the trees rustling in the wind, or a brook gurgling, or different birdies calling to one another — and

---

[2] An oat (archaic) - a musical pipe made of an oat straw, shaped like a flute.

sounded so good it all. Because of those songs, women loved Danilushko a lot. One would mend his shabby shepherd's jacket, another would cut off some canvas and sew a new shirt for him. And, of course, they would always have a treat for him, and each one would vie to give him a bigger piece and a sweeter one.

The old shepherd took a liking to Danilko's music too. But still, Danilko was not good at shepherding. Once he started playing, he would forget about the cows, you see. And that was why what happened happened.

One day Danilushko played away while the old shepherd nodded off a bit. And a few cows wandered off without notice. Only when they started home, they saw — this one is missing, that one is nowhere to be seen. They searched and searched as well as they could. But hey, you know the pasture was close to Yelnichna — a wild place it was, with wolves lurking. They found only one cow, no wonder. They led the cows home, of course, and told people what happened. The plant workers organized their search too, at once, but found nothing.

And the punishment was you know what. Whatever your fault, bare your back, yes you will! And one of the missing cows belonged to the bailiff, to boot. That one won't show you mercy, eh? They started with the old guy, but then they saw Danilko. So skinny and bony he was, even the town flogger said "This one," he said "won't last past the first time, or maybe will even give up the ghost at all."

But still he delivered the first blow, with no pity — and not a sound from Danilushko. So the flogger strikes him again, and again — but the boy is silent. And so the flogger got madder and madder and began beating him with all his might. And as he did, he would scream at the boy "I will make you cry, you brat, you'll give me a scream or two, eh?"

Danilushko is shaking like a leaf, tears in his eyes, but still not a peep — he just bites his lip and waits till it's over.

And finally he passed out, and nobody heard a peep from him. The bailiff — who was there, of course — wondered "Such spirit, this one. I know what to do with him if he lives."

Danilushko did not die. The old woman Vikhorikha put him back on his feet. There was this old one, they say. She was better than any doctor for the villagers and plant workers. They say she knew herbs, you see — which one is good for teeth, which one works for overstrain, and which will help with aches and such. She would pick those herbs herself when the best season was for each one. And then she would make potions out of roots and herbs and prepared ointments out of them.

It was good living with the old Vikhorikha. The old woman was kindly and keen to talk, and she had all those roots and herbs and dried flowers hanging about the house. Danilushko was curious about the herbs. "What is this one called? Where does it grow? What flower is that?" And the old one would tell him. Once Danilushko asked "Grandma[3], do you know every single flower that grows in our parts?"

"I am not one to boast that I know every single one," she said. "Some are open to the eye, and I know those."

And he asked "How come some are open and some are not?"

---

[3] It was common for Russian children to call all older people "grandmother" and "grandfather", and those who were their parents' age would be "auntie" or "uncle".

"Aye," she said. "Have you heard of the fern flower? You know they say it blooms on Ivanov Day[4]; that flower is magic. It opens hidden treasures. It is evil for humans, though. The fern flower is like a moving light, ghostlike. If you catch it, all locks will be open to you — a thieves' flower that is. And then there is the stone flower. It grows in the Malachite Mountain, they say. And it reaches its full power on Snakes Day. Sorry is the man who happens to see this flower."

"Why, granny, will he be sorry?"

"Ah, child, I don't know this myself, eh? People say, that's all."

Danilushko might have stayed longer with the old woman but some folks noticed he was getting better and told on him to the bailiff. And so the bailiff came to see the boy and said "Now it's time you learned the malachite craft. Go to Prokopich, that's where you belong."

What can one do? Danilushko headed for Prokopich's — and so weak he was he would sway in the wind as he went.

***

"Don't even think about it!" said Prokopich. "Even hearty ones can't stand this craft, and you are so puny you can hardly stand!"

And Prokopich went to the bailiff. "This one won't do. I might even kill him by chance — I don't need this on my conscience."

But the bailiff did not listen, you see. "I sent him to you — so your business is to teach him and that's that. This one is tough. Don't look that he is skinny and such."

---

[4] Ivanov Day is the Day of Ivan Kupala, one of the major folk holidays of the Eastern Slavs that coincides with the Christian feast of the Nativity of St. John the Baptist. It is celebrated at the end of June.

"Eh" said Prokopich. "I'll do as you say. I'll take him on but I won't answer for him to anyone."

"There is no one to answer to, eh? He is an orphan, this one, do what you will with him," the bailiff responded.

By and by, Prokopich returned home and saw Danilushko standing next to the working bench. The boy was bent over a malachite board in the cutting machine. There was a mark on the board where to cut it, and Danilo stared at that mark and shook his head. Prokopich got curious, you see, what this new boy was looking at. So he asked — sternly, in his usual manner — "What is it? Why are you holding this trick I'm working on? Who told you you can touch it?"

Danilushko said "I reckon, grandfather, that the mark is not in the right place. You see there is a pattern here, and it's going to get cut right through."

Prokopich started shouting at him, of course. "What? Who are you to judge this? A master, eh? You don't understand nothing yet."

"I understand, grandfather, that this board is ruined," says Danilushko.

"Ruined, is it? Who ruined it? You, brat, dare say this to me, first master? I'll show you "ruined"! I'll beat you black and blue so you'll be ruined yourself!"

And so he shouted and screamed, you know, but never laid a finger on Danilushko. Actually, Prokopich thought about this board a lot himself — which side to cut. So Danilushko was not wrong after all. And, when Prokopich got tired of shouting and screaming, he told the boy in a kind voice "Alright, you new master, show me how you would do it."

Danilushko began to show and explain. "You see that is how the pattern goes. And even better — if we cut it like this so it's nice and narrow — we could cut on the blank part and only leave the natural weaving on the side."

Prokopich got to shouting again. "Oh, really? Like you would know what you are talking about!" But he thought to himself "The brat talks sense, eh? He might make a good one, this boy. But how can I teach him? He'll give up the ghost from a slap or two!"

And, as he thought thus, he asked Danilo "Whose child are you, clever one?"

So Danilushko told him all about himself. An orphan he was, with no memory of his mother and, as for his father, he didn't even know his name. They called him Skinny Danilko and that's that, no last name or middle name. And he told the old man all about how he was a house boy and got kicked out and why, and about the summer when he helped the old shepherd and got beaten up for the missing cows.

Prokopich felt sorry for the boy. "Not an easy living you've had, boy, and now you are my pupil, to boot. Our craft is tough and thorough." And then it's like he got angry and grumpy. "Enough, I told you. Quite a chatterbox you are, aren't you? Talking is not working, ya know. Talk is easy, work is hard. What a pupil! I'll see tomorrow what you are good for. And now it's time to have dinner and go to sleep."

Prokopich lived alone, you see. His wife had died a long time back. An old woman called Mitrofanovna helped him about the house. She would come in the morning to cook something and to clean up, and the rest of time Prokopich did whatever he needed to keep the house by himself.

After they ate, Prokopich told the boy "Go sleep on that bench." Danilushko took off his booties, put his travel bag under his head for a pillow and covered himself with his old shepherd's jacket. Still, it was chilly in the hut, it was autumn, you see, and he shivered somewhat — but he fell asleep after all.

Prokopich went to bed too, but sleep wouldn't come to him. He kept on mulling over that malachite board. He tossed and turned and then lit up a candle and went to the cutting machine. And so he turns the board this way and that, covers one border, then the other, thinks, *a narrower cut or a wider one?* But, no matter how he turns it, the boy is right. Looks like he got the pattern better than the old master.

"This orphan, eh!" he wondered. "Hasn't even spent a day at the workshop, and tells the old master what's best. What an eye! What an eye!"

He went to the closet, found a big pillow and a huge sheepskin coat. He put the pillow under the boy's head and put the coat on top to keep him warm. "Sleep well, Sharp Eyes!"

The boy didn't even wake up, just turned on the other side, stretched under the sheepskin — warm was that coat, you see — and began to snuffle quietly. Prokopich had no kids of his own, you know, so he took this boy to heart. He stood and watched him for a while, and Danilushko just sniffled and snuffled in his sleep.

So Prokopich got to worrying how he could put the boy on his feet and make sure he was not so puny and thin. "How can he learn our trade when he is so sickly? Our dust is poison, he'll fade away quick. Let him first get some rest, put on a few, and then I'll teach him. This one will do well, I reckon."

When morning came, he told Danilushko "First, you will help me around the house. That's how things are done here. Got it? To start, go pick some guelder-rose berries. With the morning frosts like now, they will be perfect for a pie. But don't go too far, eh? Pick as many as you find, and that will be alright. Take some bread with you too — you'll get hungry in the woods — and stop by Mitrofanovna. Tell her to bake you a couple of eggs and pour you some milk. Do you understand?"

The following day he told the boy "Catch me a goldfinch chick — find a loud one — and a siskin. Make sure you bring me both by the evening. Got it?" And, when Danilushko caught the goldfinch chick and the siskin and brought them back, Prokopich said "They are alright, but I need livelier ones. Catch me more, will you?"

And it went like this for a while. Every day Prokopich would find some odd job for Danilushko, but it was all fun. When the snow set in, the old master told him to go with the neighbor — help him gather wood for the pyech[5]. But what help was that? First he would ride in the sleigh and drive the horse, and on the way back he just went behind the loaded sleigh on foot. So he would run about like this, get hungry, eat at home and sleep soundly. Prokopich had a fur coat made for him, a warm hat and mittens, and even winter booties to keep him warm in the snow.

Prokopich, you see, was a well-off man. Even if he was bonded[6], he could work for himself too, for a due, so he made some. And he took to Danilushko, you know. One could say he took him for a son. He spared nothing for the boy — but he didn't let him into his workshop yet.

Living like this, Danilushko got better fast and took to Prokopich too. Of course, he saw the old man cared for him, and it was the first time someone did. And so winter passed.

---

[5] A pyech is a heater/oven built out of brick inside a house, with a chimney leading to the roof. It served multiple functions in the household and was so large one could even sleep on top of it.
[6] Serfdom formally existed in Russia till 1861, and it took some decades for it to be fully eliminated.

Danilushko had an even better time when it did. He could run to the pond or the woods wherever his heart desired. But, still, he looked at what Prokopich did in the workshop, you see. He would hurry back home and talk to the old man. Danilushko would tell him this and that, and ask him to show how that other thing was done. Prokopich would explain and show too. And sometimes the boy would try things himself. "May I, grandpa?" And Prokopich would watch, correct him if need be and show how to better do something."

Once, the bailiff noticed Danilushko at the pond. And he asked his underlings "Whose boy is that? I see him at the pond once too often. Why is he playing with a fishing rod on a weekday? Not so little, this one — he must be put to work."

His underlings found out who the boy was and told the bailiff, but he wouldn't believe them. "Bring him in here," he said. "I'll find out for myself."

So they brought Danilushko. The bailiff asked him "Whose are you, boy?"

Danilushko told him "I am an apprentice at the malachite master's workshop."

And the bailiff took him by the ear. "You brat! That's how you are learning your craft!" And they went to Prokopich like that."

Prokopich saw how things were and tried to talk things out as well as he could. "I have sent him to catch some perches for myself. I crave fresh ones and cannot take any other food. I am unwell, you know. So I told the boy to go fishing."

The bailiff didn't believe that. And he noticed that Danilushko looked like a different boy now. He was not so skinny anymore; his shirt was new, and so were the pants and the booties. Suspicious, he decided to check

Danilushko's learning. "You tell me now what the master has taught you, eh?"

Danilushko put on an apron, came up to the stone-cutting machine and began showing him what is what. And whatever the bailiff asks about, he knows the answer — how to break stone, how to cut it, how to carve out a clean border, where and what to glue, how to polish or inlay on copper — or wood — you know, anything that a malachite master might need to do.

No matter how hard the bailiff tried to catch him on something, the boy did well. Finally, the bailiff said "So this one is better than the others, I see?"

"He is alright," said Prokopich.

"Alright, alright! But why are you spoiling him? He was sent to be your pupil and I see him at the pond with a fishing line! Watch yourself, I tell you! I'll give you some fresh perches — you'll remember till the day you die and your boy will too!"

And so he threatened them like this and left, and Prokopich wondered "When did you, Danilushko, learn all that? I haven't really taught you anything yet."

"But why, grandpa — you showed me and told me everything yourself, and I listened."

Prokopich was so touched his eyes got all red and wet. "My child," he said. "My dear Danilushko... I'll teach you everything I know. I won't hide any single thing from you."

But that was the end of the boy's easy life, eh? The bailiff sent for him the next day and began giving him trial work. First, they ordered something simple, of course: tricks like a plate for a woman's belt, jewelry boxes. But then it got to real carving like candlesticks and earrings and such. And then there was threading and engraving — leaves and petals, you know, patterns and blossoms. A malachite master's craft is like that, you see, all details.

Some little things may look like a trifle, but they will spend hours on end carving one out.

By and by, Danilushko grew up on this work.

And when he made an arm bracelet — a malachite snake he carved out of whole stone — the bailiff called him a real master after that. He even wrote to the barin about it. "I am happy to report that we have a new malachite master — Skinny Danilko. He works well, but is slow because of his young age. Shall I keep him as a 'prentice, or allow him to freelance like Prokopich does?"

Danilushko wasn't slow at all, but wonderfully fast and neat. It was Prokopich who told him to slow down. The bailiff would give Danilushko an order for five days, and Prokopich would say "This work will take two weeks, no less. He is still learning, ya know. If he rushes it, he'll only spoil good stone."

The bailiff would argue but give more days in the end. So Danilushko worked with no rush. He even learned to read and write — in secret, of course. A little bit, sure, but something is better than nothing. Prokopich encouraged him too. He even tried to help him with the bailiff's orders, but Danilushko wouldn't let him. "What gives, Papa? Why would you sit at the machine in my stead? Look how your beard is all green from all that malachite work, and your health is not the same. And I am young and fit, ain't I?"

Danilushko got strong and handsome by then for real. They still called him Skinny, but he was not that at all! Tall he was, with a healthy blush on his cheeks, a head full of blond curls, and jolly, to boot. Girls would pine for him, no wonder here. And Prokopich got to talking to him about a bride, but Danilushko would shake his fair head and say "Don't rush me, Papa. Let me become a real master first, then I'll think about it."

***

The barin wrote back to the bailiff. "I want this Prokopich's apprentice Danilko to carve a stone vase with a stem and a base for my household. Then I will decide if I can allow him to freelance or keep him under the old master. But you should watch the boy to make sure Prokopich does not help him in any way. If you overlook something, you'll have to answer for that."

The bailiff read the letter, called for Danilushko and said "You will work here, not at Prokopich's workshop. We will bring in a machine for you and any stone you need."

Prokopich was real upset when he found out. "How come? Why?" He even went to the bailiff but the bailiff would not even talk to him. He just shouted at the old man. "None of your business what I do!"

Danilushko went to work in the new place, and Prokopich told him "Look, Danilushko, keep your pace, don't rush — don't show what you can do."

Danilushko remembered what Prokopich said at first. He would take a measure and think about this way and that, to start with, but got bored, in the end. Whether you do it or not, you still have to sit indoors from morning till night, eh? So, because he was bored, he showed his true speed and strength. He finished the barin's goblet, the bailiff looked it over and told him "Make another one like this, will ya?"

Danilushko made another one, then another one yet. And, when he was done with this third, the bailiff said "Gotcha! Now you can't back out of work. Our barin gave you time for one goblet, and you carved out three in that time. Now I know how you really work. You can't pretend anymore, and I will teach that old dog how to lie to me! He'll remember till the end of his days!"

And that's what he wrote to the barin, sending all three cups that Danilko made. But the barin — who knows why, maybe he wanted to show how smart he was, or he was angry at the bailiff for some reason — decided quite the opposite.

He asked for a small due from Danilo's freelancing, and ordered to keep the boy at Prokopich's. "Maybe they will think up something new together, those two," he wrote.

The barin attached a drawing to his letter. The drawing was that of a vase with different trifles carved on it, with patterned borders, a winding stone band and some leaves on the base. And the note on the drawing was this: "Let him spend as long as five years on it if he needs — I want a vase exactly like this".

And so the bailiff had to go back on his threat. He said that the barin's wish was to let Danilko freelance at Prokopich's workshop. And that the barin wanted a vase like in the drawing.

Danilushko and Prokopich were real glad about this news, and they got to work with zest. Danilushko started thinking about how to make the new vase. Lots of complex stuff there was about it. If you strike in the wrong place, the stone is ruined and you have to start from scratch. But Danilushko's eye was sharp, his hand was steady and his strength was just right, so the work went well.

Still, there was something not to his liking. Lots of work that vase was, you see, but not much beauty in it. He even said this to Prokopich, but the old master just wondered at him in surprise "What's that to you? They drew it like so — we'll carve it this way. You know how many tricks like this I've carved — and what for? I have no idea."

Danilo tried talking to the bailiff, but no. The man just stamped his feet and waved his hands at him. 'Have you lost your mind? This drawing cost the barin a lot. It was probably made by the first artist in the capital — and who are you to judge!"

And then he recalled the barin's words — *maybe they'll think up something new together* — and he said "You know what? You carve this vase according to the barin's drawing, but, if you wish to carve another one for yourself, it's up to you. I won't meddle with that. We have enough stone for that too. Whichever one you need, I'll send it to the workshop."

So Danilushko got to thinking about it. You know what they say: it's easy to point out what's wrong with others' work; much harder it is to think up something new yourself — you'll spend nights tossing and turning over it.

Danilushko would sit at the machine working on the barin's vase but thinking about something else. He would try in his head which flower and which leaf would be more suitable for which stone. Thoughtful he became, and glum. Prokopich noticed that and asked "Are you feeling ill, Danilushko? Take it easy on that vase, eh? No rush with it, remember? Go take a walk. You sit and sit for hours on end, that won't do."

"Why not?" thought Danilushko. "I might as well go out for a bit. Maybe I'll see in the woods what I need." And so he would take walks in the woods almost every day since then. It was harvest season, lots of berries everywhere — and all our grasses were in bloom. Danilushko would sometimes stop at a meadow and stare at the grass and flowers like he lost something.

Lots of people were in the meadows and fields those days. They would ask him "What did you lose, Danilushko?" And he would smile a sad smile and answer "It's not that I lost anything, but I can't find what I'm looking for."

Some even started whispering behind his back "Something's wrong with the boy."

Danilo, though, would come home from those walks and sit at his working table at once — till the wee hours — and then again would head for the forest or the meadows. He would bring leaves and flowers home, strange, unwanted ones mostly — hellebore and hemlock, nightshade and wild rosemary, and other weeds like that.

He got thin in the face, and his eyes had no rest, while his hand lost its strength. Prokopich got worried about him, and Danilo told him "Can't stop thinking about that vase, you know. I want to carve it in such a way as to show the stone's full strength and beauty."

Prokopich tried to talk him out of it. "What do you need it for? We don't go hungry, what more? The noble ones can amuse themselves how they like — if they just let us be. They will think up a trick and we'll make it. Why do something more than that? You'll call a new yoke on our heads, will you?"

But Danilushko didn't give in. "This one is not for the barin. I just can't forget about *my* vase, you know. Look at the stone we have — such stone! And what do we do with it? We cut it and carve it, and polish it — but it's all for nothing. And I want to make something so as to see the real strength of our stone — and show it to people too."

By and by, Danilushko got back to the barin's vase. He would cut and carve and chuckle to himself. "A stone band with drilled holes in it, and a winding border, ha! What do they know?"

And then he stopped his work again, and started a different vase. He spent whole days and nights at his machine. And he said to Prokopich "I am going to use nightshade as a model."

Prokopich tried to get him away from that vase again, and Danilushko would not listen. But, in the end, when something didn't go as he wanted, he told Prokopich "Be it your way. I'll finish the barin's vase first, and then go back to mine. But when I do, don't talk me out of it no more — I can't get it out of my head."

Prokopich said then "Alright, I won't bother you," but he thought to himself *"Maybe he'll forget about it as time goes by. He needs a wife, he does, that's it. He won't have time for this silliness when he has a family."*

***

Danilushko got back to working on the barin's order. Hard work it was, no less than a couple of years. He worked like that for a while, and didn't think about his own project. Prokopich started talking to him about a wife. "Why don't you ask Katya Letemina? She would make a proper one. Such a girl she is! No one can find a bad word to say about her."

Prokopich had a good reason to talk about Katya. He noticed a long time ago that Danilushko couldn't take his eyes off the girl. And she didn't seem to mind. So Prokopich mentioned her in passing — like he didn't know anything. And Danilushko would nod at his work "Hold up, Papa. Let me finish this vase. I am sick and tired of it — so sick I could smash it with a hammer and be done with it. Don't even mention a wedding now. Katya and I have an agreement already. She will wait."

By and by Danilushko finished the barin's vase at last. The bailiff, of course, wasn't told about it just yet, but they decided to celebrate it at home with a small party of friends. Katya, the bride, came with her parents and then some malachite carvers were invited as well.

Katya looked at the vase and wondered "Such an intricate pattern, Danilushko, how did you manage to carve it out and not break any of the stone — it's all so smooth and cleanly cut and polished!"

The masters nodded their approval too. "Exact like the drawing, no fault can be found; so cleanly made — couldn't be done better or faster. If you keep working like this, we won't catch up with you."

Danilushko listened to all this and said "That's just what is wrong — nothing to find fault with. It's all smooth and clean, and the pattern is like it should be, and the carvings are exactly like in the drawing. But where is beauty? Take a flower — any meadow flower, or a weed. You look at it and your heart leaps with joy. And who will be joyful looking at this one? What is it for? Some will wonder like Katyenka, at the master's eye and at his hand, and how he had patience enough to carve it all out and never break the stone…"

"And, if you might have," the masters laughed "you glued it back together and polished it so well nobody would know, eh?"

"Right, right! But where is the beauty of the stone, I say? Here is a vein in the malachite, but the drawing says there should be holes and flowers where it lies. What are they for, I ask? We just spoil stone like this. And such stone, you see? First-rate stone, with natural patterns." So his speech got all heated. He had a drink or two, no surprise there.

And the masters told Danilushko what Prokopich said many times "Stone is stone. What do you want from it? Our job is to cut it and carve it, and that's that."

But there was this little old guy there, you see. He was a stone master long before Prokopich and others came of age. And everyone called him Grandpa. Very frail and old he was, but he understood what the talk was about and said "Sweet child, Danilo, get such notions out of your head, will ya? Walking on the edge you are now, with thoughts like this. The Lady will take you as her mountain master."

"Why, Grandpa? What are those masters?"

"They are... Nobody knows what or who they are. They live in the mountain and do whatever the Lady tells them to. I saw their work once — such mastery! Differs from ours in everything!"

Everybody got curious, o'course, and they asked him "What did you see, Grandpa?"

And he told them "I saw a snake, ya know, like the ones you make for an arm bracelet."

"So what?" They snickered. "What's so special about a snake armlet?"

"Different it was from ours, ya see. Any master will say it was not made by one of our own. Our snakes are made of stone, even if pretty, but that one — like it was alive, with a dark gray spine and the eyes — like it'd jump at you any moment. Those masters, they saw the *stone flower*, they know what beauty is."

Danilushko perked up when he heard about the stone flower and tried to find out more. But the little old master said earnestly "I don't know, sweet child. I have heard about this flower but it is no good for us people. If one sees it, one won't care for anything anymore."

Danilushko told him anyway "I would give anything to see it, Grandpa."

So his bride, Katyenka, she got all upset. "Come come, Danilushko, are you so tired of our life here?" And she started crying.

Prokopich and the other masters saw what is what and thought to make a fool out of the old guy. "You are out of your mind, Grandpa. What fairytales you tell. Just leading the young guy astray, are ya?"

But the little old master got all red and hot. "The stone flower is no fairytale. The boy is right — we don't understand stone. That flower shows its true beauty."

And the masters just snorted at him. "You've had one too many, Grandpa!"

But still he insisted "No fairytale is the stone flower. It is real as real and that's that."

***

When the guests left, Danilo wouldn't leave alone what the old master said. He got to taking long walks in the forest again, would look at that nightshade flower for hours — and forgot to think about the wedding. Prokopich began talking to him about it. "Why do you bring the girl to shame? How long will she go about unwed? People are going to start laughing at her. Lots of gossips' tongues we have in the village, ya know."

But Danilushko gave him the same answer. "Wait a bit, grandpa. When I figure out the stone I need and get it..."

And so he would head again to the copper mine — Gumeshki it was called. Sometimes he would go into the mine and walk about the downholes, and sometimes he would look at the stones people brought up. Once he picked up a stone, looked at it and said to himself "Neah, this one won't do..."

And, no sooner had he said that, someone told him "Look in a different place — around Snakes Mountain."

Danilushko looked around but didn't see a soul. *"What the heck?"* He thinks. *"Somebody's pulling a trick on me or what?"*

He looked around once more but, just as he started home, he heard the same voice again. "Do you hear, Danilo-master? Told ya, Snakes Mountain is the place."

Danilo turned around and saw a woman like blue mist. And then nothing at all.

"What was that?" he thought. *"Was that the Lady herself? Maybe I should go to Snakes Mountain, eh?"*

He knew Snakes Mountain well, o'course. It was a spot not far from Gumeshki. But it wasn't really a mountain anymore; it got all mined inside out.

Danilo went to that mountain the following day. It wasn't much of a mountain, true, but still quite steep. One side was all open from the mining, you know, so you could see all the layers and which stone was where — first-rate stone, for sure!

Danilushko came closer to the vertical cut and saw a huge slab of malachite. The stone was so big you couldn't pick it up and take it home — and sort of looked like a bush or some other plant. Danilushko stared at the find from all angles. Everything was like he needed: the color was deeper at the bottom, the veins were where he wanted them... Just what was needed for his purposes.

Danilushko, happy, ran to find a cart and a horse, brought the stone home and showed it to Propokyich. "Look, Papa! This stone is perfect for my work! I will start and finish it in no time now! And then we'll have the wedding! Right you are, Katyenka has waited for me too long. But it hasn't been easy for me — this work won't let me go. Can't wait to be done with it!"

That's when Danilushko really got to working on that flower of his. He would cut and carve the stone day and night. Prokopich would keep his mouth shut too. He thought maybe the lad would calm down when he had his fill. The work was fast. The bottom of the stone got finished quickly. And it really looked like a nightshade bush you see. Dark-green leaves in a bunch, pointed, with veins — a perfect pattern he found for that.

Prokopich said "Your flower is like a real one, even to the touch." But when Danilo reached the top, he got stuck like. He cut and polished the stem and the side petals — so fine was his carving, one wondered how it all held together! Then he started on the cup of the flower — but no... It still looked like a nightshade but it was not a live one anymore. And not beautiful.

Danilushko lost his sleep. He would sit around the vase and mull over how to make it right or what to change. Prokopich and the other masters would drop by and marvel. "What else does he want? The vase is like nothing anyone has seen before, and still he thinks it's not good enough. The guy is not right in the head and needs the old Vikhorikha or other such help."

Katyenka heard what people were saying and started crying. This, finally, put Danilushko back on the ground.

"Alright," he said. "I'm done with this vase. It looks like I cannot carve so that the strength of stone can be really seen. I have no real understanding of its beauty... Let's hurry up with that wedding, eh?"

But what hurry when the bride had prepared everything a long time ago! They set the day, and Danilushko got his good spirits back.

And so he told the bailiff about that vase, you see. The bailiff came running and stared at it in wonder. Such an amazing trick was that vase. He wanted to send the vase to the barin at once but Danilyshko told him "Hold on a bit, I need to finish something up."

***

It was autumn, and the wedding was set for Snakes Day. So somebody mentioned that on that day all snakes would gather in one place. Danilushko noted that word and remembered the little old master's talk about the stone flower. And he felt the pull of Snakes Mountain, you see, and thought *"Maybe I should go there one last time? Someone helped me there once, didn't she?"* He thought of the stone. "That stone was like someone put it there for *me. And that voice at the copper mine... that told me to go to Snakes Mountain..."*

He went to the mountain thinking so. There was frost on the ground by then, and it was snowing a bit. He came to that mined place where he found the stone and saw a huge hollow in the mountain side like someone had been mining there. He did not think about who that could be but decided to hide from the wind and rest a little in that very spot.

He went into the cave and saw a gray boulder like a chair. So he sat down on it and stared at the ground as he thought his thoughts about the stone flower. *"If only I could see it,"* he thought. And he felt warm all of a sudden, like summer was back again.

Danilushko raised his head and saw a woman on the other side of the hollow. He knew the Lady at once — only she alone could be so beautiful, and that liquid malachite dress could only be hers. But then he thought *"I am probably seeing things; there is nobody there."* So he sat and didn't say a word, and looked where she stood like there was nothing there.

She was quiet too, like thinking about something, but then she said "So, Master Danilo, that malachite flower of yours won't come out right, eh?"

"Neah," he said. "It won't."

"Don't lose heart just yet. Try something new. You'll find stone when you think something up."

"No," he told her. "I can't stand It anymore. I have exhausted myself, but I just can't do it. Show me the stone flower, Lady, I beg ya."

"I could show it to you," she answered. "But you will regret it."

"Will you keep me in the mountain?"

"Why would I?" she said. "I am not keeping anybody. The way is open, but they come back anyway."

"Please, Lady, show it to me."

She kept on talking him out of it, though. "Try doing something yourself, eh? And think about Prokopich, he didn't spare himself for you; why do you want to leave him now? And your bride? She has given you all her heart, and yours is set on other things."

"I know, I know!" Danilushko cried out. "But I can't live without seeing that flower. Please show me!"

"Well, so be it then, Master Danilo," she said. "Come to my garden."

She said that and rose from where she sat. There was a rustle, like the sound of ground sliding. Danilushko looked around but there were no more stone walls. He saw awesome trees, tall and not like the ones in our woods — they were cut in stone, you see. Some were marble, some were serpentine. But they were living trees, with branches, twigs and leaves. They swayed in the wind and there was a ringing sound like someone was playing with pebbles.

The ground was covered with grass, also made of stone — some blades were blue, some red and other colors. There was no sun but the light was like it was just before sunset. In between those trees he saw some shiny golden snakes hopping around, playing. "So that's where the light comes from," he reckoned.

The woman brought Danilushko to a big clearing. The ground there looked like regular clay, with bushes growing out of it like black velvet. And there were green bell flowers on those bushes, carved from malachite, and each had a tiny silver star inside. Some fiery bees flew about those flowers, and the little stars rang like they were singing a song.

"Well, Danilo-master, have you seen enough?" the Lady asked.

"But there is no such stone," he replied "to carve this beauty out of."

"If you thought it up yourself, I would give you any stone — but I can't now!"

And, as she said that, she waved her hand. There was rustling again, and Danilo found himself on the same gray boulder in the hollow. A strong cold wind was blowing, the way it does in autumn.

***

Danilushko returned home, and he was just in time for Katyenka's brides party. He appeared merry at first — sang songs, danced even — but then he got thoughtful and somber. The bride got all worried. "What's up with you, dear love? You look like you are at a funeral."

And he answered "My head hurts, that's why. I see black and green and red. Can't see the light no more."

That's when the party ended, of course. Like the custom was, the bride and her mates went to see the groom off. But the road was short — his house was a stone's throw from hers. So Katya thought of something.

"Let's go the long way around, my friends. We can go down our street till the very end, and then come back by Yelanskaya." And she thought to herself *"Maybe the fresh air will do good to Danilushko."*

And her mates were happy anyway. "Sure," they laughed. "We need to see him off properly. He lives too close. We have never even sung a farewell song to see him off as we should."

The night was quiet, and a light snow was falling — no better time to go for a walk. So they went — the bride and the groom at the front, and her mates with a bachelor who was at the party too a little behind. And the girls started their farewell song which was sad and slow, like to see off a dead one.

Katyenka noticed that was not good. *"Danilushko is gloomy already, and they are wailing like this,"* she thought.

She tried to turn Danilushko's mind away from dark thoughts. And he'd talk to her some but then shut down again. The bride's mates finished the sad song and got to singing something cheery at last. And so they laughed, and ran around, and Danilushko walked with his head down, and Katyenka couldn't do anything to change his mood.

Finally, they reached his house. Their companions left, and Danilushko went to see his bride off — no such custom, but he did it anyway.

***

When he came home, Prokopich had gone to sleep already. Danilushko lit a candle, dragged his vases in the middle of the living room and stared at them. Prokopich had a coughing fit at that time. He coughed and coughed like he would spit his lungs out — and he wouldn't stop.

That cough cut Danilushko's heart like a knife. Prokopich, you see, by then got to be very unwell. Danilushko remembered their life together and felt very sorry for the old master.

Prokopich — when he stopped coughing — finally asked him "What's up with the vases, eh?"

"Just thinking, maybe it's time we sent them off."

"It's high time," Prokopich said. "They just take up space here, and you won't make them any better anyway."

They talked a bit like this, and Prokopich fell back asleep. Danilushko went to bed too, but sleep wouldn't come. He tossed and turned, then got up, lit up a candle again, looked at the vases, and came up to Prokopich. And he sighed and sighed as he stood by the old man.

And then he took a hammer and smashed his nightshade flower — just a loud crack and that's all. But the other vase, the one he made for the barin, that one he didn't touch — he just spat in the middle of it and ran out of the hut. Since then, nobody saw him or heard of him.

Some said he lost his mind and found his end in the woods, but then others would say that the Lady took him on as her mountain master.

That's not how it turned out but this is a story for another evening.

The Stone Master

Katya, Danilo's bride, remained unmarried. Two or three years after Danilo disappeared she wasn't even in a bride's age anymore. If you are over twenty years old here in the village, you are too old already, that's what we say here. Such girls would rarely get a young guy for a husband — a widower, mayhap.

Katya was real pretty though, so lots of men came to ask for her hand, even when her age was not proper any more. But she had one answer, "I am promised to Danilo."

And they would tell her "So you were. But nothing has come out of it, eh? Why would you remember that? Dead is dead."

But she would stand her ground. "I am betrothed to him. Perhaps he'll come back still."

Our village folk tried to talk sense into her. "He must be dead. Why else would he not be here now?"

But she wouldn't budge. "No one has seen him dead so he is alive to me."

People saw the girl didn't have all her wits about her, and they left her alone. Some even started to mock her. They called her a deadman's bride. And she was fine with that. Katya, Deadman's bride — that was her new name, and she didn't mind.

A plague came about around that time, and Katya's mum and pop both passed away. She did have some relations: three married brothers and some unmarried sisters. So they had a quarrel about who would stay in the parents' house. Katya saw that nothing good would come out of it and said "I will go live at Danilo's place. Prokopich is too old to take care of himself. I'll look after him."

The siblings got to talking her out of it. "That won't do, dear Katya. He is old, of course, but you never know what people might say."

"What do I care?" she said. "I am not the one to gossip. Prokopich is family. He was adopted father to my Danilo. I'll call him Father."

And so she left. The relatives didn't argue much against it. They thought to themselves "One less mouth to think about". And Prokopich? He was glad she came to stay. "Thank you, Katyenka, for thinking about me, my dear child."

They started living together like that. Prokopich spent days and nights at the carving table, and Katya would help about the house — mind the garden, cook meals and other stuff. Not much to do for the two of them, and she was a quick one, so it was no trouble at all for her. She would finish her housekeeping and get to her needlework — whatever needed to be done, the sewing or the knitting. And it all went well at first. But then Prokopich became unwell. He would sit up one day and lie in bed the other two. He had worked too much, you see, and was getting on in years. Katya got to thinking how they were going to live from then on. *"Needlework is not enough to live on... and I don't know any other craft,"* she thought.

So she says to Prokopich "Father, maybe you could teach me some simple thing or two."

Prokopich even got a laugh out of it. "What? It's not a girl's job to carve malachite. Never heard of a thing like that."

But she began to keep an eye on his craft and would help him when she could — file something off or polish, you know. Prokopich saw she was getting the hang of it and started to show her some tricks too. Nothing too serious — just how to carve out a buckle or attach handles to forks and spoons — the little things that were ordered most often, trifles and not much money to make on but still a bit of extra income.

Prokopich did not live long. And afterwards Katya's siblings got to pestering her about finding a man again. "You have to, now. How else will you live all by your lonesome?"

Katya cut them off. "None of your business that is. I don't need a groom. Danilo will come back, I know it. He is in the mountain, studying his craft. When he's done, he'll return."

So the siblings waved their hands at her. "Are you out of your mind, Katerina? It's a sin to even mention his name. He is long dead, your Danilo, and she is still waiting… You are going to start seeing things soon.

And she said "I don't fear that."

So they asked "What will you live on?"

And she replied "Don't you worry about that either. I will be alright."

The siblings made it out that Prokopich left some moneys to her, and got back to their pestering. "How come you are such a fool! If you do have some money, you sure need a man to take care of the house. Someone might be tempted to come and rob you of it otherwise. They'll wring your neck like a chicken's. You won't even know it."

"Whatever I am destined to live, I'll live it out on my own," she answered.

So her relatives made some more noise — some shouted at her, others cried. But Katya stood her ground. "I'll hold out by myself, no need for any other groom. I have Danilo."

Her relations got mad at her, o'course. "Don't even show your face if need be."

"Thank you very much, my dear brothers and sisters. I will remember your words. And neither do you. Don't knock on my door when you pass my hut." And she laughed. The siblings left and banged the door behind them.

***

She was left all alone and tears came to her eyes. She cried at first but then said "Nope, I won't give in to this."

She wiped off her tears and decided to clean up. She would scrub and wash and dust around. And when she finished, she sat at the carving machine. She also tidied up a bit there, the way she wanted things. She put aside what she didn't need, and placed other things close at hand. Having put things in order, she decided to try doing something all by herself at the machine.

"I'll try to carve a belt buckle first," she thought.

But, when she looked around, she didn't see any proper stone for that. She still had the pieces from Danilo's nightshade vase, of course, but she was saving them. Prokopich had a lot of stone for sure. But he worked big projects ever till he died. So none of the slabs he had were the proper size. And the little pieces and shards were all gone. They had already used them for the small tricks they made together.

Finally, she thought *"I should probably go look around the mine. There may be some fitting stone for me there."* She remembered from both Danilo and Prokopich that Snakes Mountain was a good spot. So she went there.

She had to pass Gumeshki on her way there, and lots of people were there, some sorting the ore, some loading it on carts. And they all saw her pass with a basket. She did not care much to be ogled like that, so she went around the hill to look for her stone on the other side. She had to pass through some dense forest as she went up Snakes

Mountain. When she reached the top, she sat down for a bit. She felt sad and missed Danilo so much.

And so she sat on a stone and her tears fell to the ground. There was no one to see her, just the trees all around and she had her guard down like that.

A little later she looks down at her feet and sees a malachite stone on the ground — but it's deep and she can't take it out. How can she get at it with no pickaxe or some other tool?

Still, she tried to move it with her hand. And it turned out to be sitting quite loose. She began to dig the soil around it with a pine stick and then got to rocking it back and forth. Something crunched — like a branch snapping — and she was holding it in her hands.

The stone wasn't big, and flat it was, like a bar, maybe three fingers thick, as wide as a palm and around a foot in length. She looked at it in wonder.

"Just what I need, eh? I'll file it and make a bunch or buckles with it — with minimal losses."

She brought the stone home and got to preparing it for the job she had in mind. The work was slow, and she also needed to take care of the household. So she was busy all day long, with no time to spare. And, as she sat at the carving machine, she would remember Danilushko. *"I wish he could see the new master we have here, sitting in his and Prokopich's place!"*

***

And, of course, there were the bullies. Every village has some, right? One night, as she sat late, busy working, three men climbed over her fence and into the yard. Who knows what they wanted — just to scare her or something more — drunk they were, of course. She was filing and didn't hear them enter the mudroom. She only heard them when they started banging on the main door.

"Hey you, Deadman's Bride! Open up. You have some live guests now!"

She first tried to talk to them. "Hey guys, you'd better leave, eh?"

But they wouldn't listen. They kept ramming her door so hard it would break soon. So she took the hook off, opened it wide and screamed at them "Come in, you guests! Who's the first one to get hacked, tell me?"

They look and see she is holding an axe.

"Stop your jokes, will you?" they say.

And she answers "What jokes? Whoever comes in will get the axe's treat!"

The men — even if drunk — saw that she was not kidding. She was a big girl, with wide shoulders, and the look in her eyes! Besides, she knew how to hold that axe, for sure.

So they didn't dare come in. They screamed and shouted some but then left and told everyone what happened. They were even teased afterwards — three big guys and got scared of one girl. They didn't have much liking for that, o'course. So they said there was a deadman standing behind her; that's why they ran.

"He was such a creep, you would run too," they said.

Whether they were believed or not, people started saying things like "Something's not right with that house. There is a reason she lives all alone there."

Katya heard that gossip but didn't lose much sleep over it. She even thought *"Let them talk. Even better if they fear coming here. They will let me be next time around."*

The neighbors were also amazed at her sitting at the machine, of course. They started mocking her for it. "What is she thinking? Trying to do a man's job, is she? Huh!"

This she liked less. She had her own doubts, you see. *"Will I manage it all on my own?"* she wondered. But then she collected herself. *"Just commonplace trifles, right? As long as they are polished right, I can make those for sure!"*

She cut that stone she found into several parts and saw that the pattern was rare and just what she wanted for her tricks. It's like there were even marks for her where to carve what.

She did wonder how easy things seemed to be going for her. She cut the parts into slices, the shape she needed and began carving them out. It wasn't hard but tricky enough without much practice. She had difficulty at first but then got the hang of things. The buckles were good indeed, and not much stone was lost. The only waste was what she had to carve away.

She made a lot of those tricks, wondered again at how good the stone turned out to be and got to thinking about selling what she made.

Prokopich used to take such small trifles to town, where he had a guy he knew who ran a shop. She had heard about that shop many times. So she took it to mind to go to town. *"I'll ask him — for the future — if he would take my stuff should I bring him more,"* she thought.

She locked the hut and went on foot. They didn't even notice her leave in Polevaya.

***

Once she got to town, she asked around about where the shop was, found it and went to see that guy. When she entered, she saw so many different stones and lots of buckles too — a whole glass case with shelves full of them. There were many people at the shop, some buying and others selling. And the owner looked so important and serious.

At first she was even afraid to come up to him and ask but she finally gathered her courage. "Would you be willing to buy some belt buckles from me, by any chance?"

He pointed to the glass case. "See how many I have already?"

And the carvers who stood by said "So much stone is wasted on these trifles, eh? Some folks just don't get it that a good pattern is needed to make a proper buckle."

And one of those carvers was from Polevaya. He whispered to the owner "This girl, she is not all there, eh? Our neighbors saw her at the cutting machine. Let's see what nonsense she cooked."

So the owner said "OK, show me what you've got."

Katya gave him a buckle. He stared at it, then at Katya, and said "Who did you steal it from?"

She got upset, of course. She talked different to the owner then. "What right do you have to talk about a person like that when you know nothing about them? Look here if you ain't blind. Where would I steal such a lot of buckles like this — with one pattern? See?" and she spilled all her tricks onto the counter.

Both the owners and the carvers saw that what she said was true — the pattern was one and the same. And a rare pattern it was: like there was a tree in the middle, and a bird sitting on its top branch and another bird below. Everything could be seen clearly and carved properly.

The buyers overheard that talk and drew nearer to see what is what, but the owner covered the belt buckles at once. He even found an excuse. "You won't see much like this. I'll put them into the glass case, one by one, and then you'll choose which you like best."

He turned to Katya. "You go into that other room, you'll get your money there." She went where he pointed, and the owner followed. "How much do you want?" he asked.

Katya heard which prices are good from Prokopich and Danilo, and she told him how much. He laughed. "What? Are you for real? I only paid this much to Prokopich and his adopted pupil Danilo. Such masters they were!"

"That's where I know which price to ask. I am from that family too."

"Ah!" the owner started. "So that's where these buckles come from — left from those two."

"No," she said. "It's my work."

"Mayhap the stone was chosen by one of them?"

"I have found that stone myself."

The owner didn't believe her, she saw, but Katya decided not to argue about it. He gave her what she had asked and even told her "If you happen to make something like this again, bring it to me. I'll take it and give you a good price."

Katya was glad to get so much money. And, after she had left, the owner laid out those buckles in his glass case. The buyers flocked in. 'How much?" They asked.

And he, knowing their worth, put the tenfold price for those tricks, saying "We haven't seen such a pattern yet. It's the work of Danilo from Polevaya. Nobody can do better than him."

On her way back Katya wondered *"How did this happen? My buckles turned out to be the best in that shop. Such a lucky stone I found!"* She came home and couldn't help thinking *"Maybe it was Danilo's way to say he is alright?"*

And, as she thought so, she ran out of her house.

***

One of our carvers — the one who wanted to make fun of her in the shop — came back home to Polevaya and started mulling things over. *"I need to see where she gets her stone from. Maybe Prokopyich or Danilo showed her some new place."*

So he noticed Katya run off somewhere and followed her. He saw that she went around Gumeshki and headed for Snakes Mountain. He did the same. *"The forest is dense there,"* he thought. *"I'll sneak behind her so she won't even notice I'm there."*

They entered the forest like that. Katya doesn't know someone is following her so she doesn't look around and goes without fear. The carver is gleeful, you know, that he'll see the new place so easily.

Suddenly, he heard a strange hum to the side — so strange he stood still in fright. He stopped to listen and see what's up. And, while he looked around, he lost Katya's trail. He ran and ran around the forest for hours but couldn't find his way back. He finally ran out to Seversky pond — a couple of miles from Gumeshki.

Katya didn't even have a thought someone might be trying to follow her. She climbed up the mountain where she had found that first stone. She saw that the hole she dug got a bit bigger somehow, and there is another stone on the side. She rocked it around and set it free. Like the last time, something crunched like a twig.

She took the stone in her hands and began to weep and mumble whichever words she found — like village women would when there is a deadman in the house. "Why oh why did you leave me my sweet friend, my sweetheart!" and so on and so forth.

She cried to her heart's desire and felt somewhat better. She stood and looked towards the ore mine. She noticed a spot like a clearing. There was a forest around it, dense at first and then less thick towards where the ore mine was. It was dusk, you know. The sun was setting down, and its rays slid by that clearing. And it seemed like that clearing was on fire so many stones glittered in the sun.

Katya got curious, of course. She wanted to come closer so she stepped forward. There was a crunch. Startled, she put her foot back and saw there was no ground where she was going to step at all.

She found herself standing on a tall tree, on one of its top branches. There were other trees like that all around her, with pointed tops. And in between the trees she could see some flowers and grasses — and all unfamiliar, not from around here.

Another girl would be full of fright, would start screaming, but Katya's mind was on something else. *"Ah, the mountain has opened up! Mayhap I'll see my Danilushko!"*

And, just as she thought that, she saw someone approaching, down below, who looked like Danilo — and this person raised his arms towards her like he wanted to say something. Katya rushed to him without thinking — but she was up in that tree! So she fell to the ground where she had stood before.

She came to her senses and said "Must have been seeing things. Better go home now."

She knew she had to go but still lingered at the mountain top, waiting — maybe it would open again and show her Danilushko. And she sat like that till twilight. But, as she was returning home, she thought *"I did see Danilo, didn't I?"*

***

The carver — the one who had followed her earlier — he came home before her. He checked on her hut when he did, but it was locked at that time. He decided to hide and wait. "I'll see what she brings," he mumbled.

And so, when he saw Katya, he stood in front of her, barring her way.

"Where did you go?" he asked.

"To Snakes Mountain," she said.

"What did you do there at night, eh?"

"I went to visit Danilo, that's what."

The carver stepped back in shock. And the next day people started to whisper "The Deadman's bride did lose her mind, eh? Going to Snakes mountain to wait for her dead groom. What if she takes it into her head to burn the plant down or something?"

Her siblings heard that gossip and came to warn and talk her off. But she wouldn't listen. She just showed them the money and said "Where do you think this came from? Even good masters can't sell their tricks, and this is what I got the first time I made something by myself! Why is that, you think?"

Her brothers heard what she said and answered "You got lucky, baby sister. Nothing to talk about."

"People don't just get lucky like this. Danilo himself chose that pattern and put that stone out for me."

The siblings laughed at her and waved their hands. "You are out of your mind indeed! We need to tell the bailiff in case she does do something crazy!"

They told him nothing, of course. They didn't want to betray their sister. But when they left her house they agreed to check in on her, just in case. "Let's see where she goes and follow her, to be on the safe side."

Katya saw them off and took to cutting the new stone. And as she worked on it she thought *"If this stone is as good as the one before, I wasn't seeing things. Danilo was there for sure!"*

And so she didn't want to stop till she finished the cut. She couldn't wait to see what pattern she would get. Night fell, but she was still at the carving machine.

One of her sisters woke up, saw the light in Katya's windows and sneaked to see what was up. She looked through the window and wondered *"What is going on with this girl? Does she ever sleep? Why is she so odd, this one?"*

Katya finally finished cutting her stone and saw the pattern, even more beautiful than before. The bird that had been at the top of the tree took off to fly down, and the one at the bottom of the tree spread its wings and was flying up. This pattern was repeated five times on the malachite board. And, again, it was like there were marks on the board on how to cut it across.

Katya didn't even stop to think. She just rushed out of the hut and ran. Her sister rushed after her — but, while she did, she knocked on the brothers' doors. "Come join me".

They ran out and found some more people to join them. It was dawn by then so they saw her run past Gumeshki. They all rushed to catch up and see where she would go, and she didn't even feel someone was after her.

She ran by the ore mine and went at a slower pace to go around Snakes mountain. The crowd that followed slowed down too — to see what happens next.

Katya walked up the mountain as was her habit by now. By and by, she looked around and found herself in a strange forest. Amazed, she touched a tree with the palm of her hand. The trunk is cold and smooth, like it's polished stone. And the grass below her feet is made of stone, it seems like, and it's still dark in here. So Katya thinks "I must be inside the mountain now, that's why."

Her relatives and other folks got alarmed. "Where did she go? She was right here!" So they fussed and ran around — some up the mountain, some down the mountain — calling to each other "Can you see her? Is she there?"

Meanwhile, Katya roamed about the stone forest thinking how to find Danilo. After walking around like this, she decided to call for him "Danilo, where are you? Danilo, hey!"

And she heard some echoes "Nay, nay..."

But she hollered again. "Danilo, hey! Danilo!"

Suddenly, a woman stood in front of her — the Lady of the Mountain herself.

"Why are you here in my forest, girl?" the Lady said. "What do you want? Looking for some good stones, are you? Take any you like and just get out of here."

And Katya tells her "I don't want your dead stone. I want my Danilo, alive and well. Bring him forth, will you? Where do you hide him? He is not your groom so let him be!"

Such boldness from a common girl! Unheard of to say words like this to the Lady herself! But the Lady stood calmly and asked her "Anything else you want to tell me?"

"That is what I am telling you: give me back my Danilo!"

The Lady burst out laughing "You fool, do you know who it is you are speaking to?"

"I am not blind," Katya said. "I see who you are. But I am not afraid of you, you homewrecker! Not a tiny bit! Sly you are, but Danilo wants to reach out to me anyway. I saw that with my own eyes! What do you say now?"

The Lady listened to her and said "Let's hear him out, shall we?"

It had been dark in the forest but now it got all lit up. It was light like daytime. The grass shone in different colors, and Katya saw that those trees were all so pretty. She could see a clearing in between their branches, and there were flowers in that clearing, with golden bees flying around them like sparkles. Such beauty that was — one couldn't but gaze at it all in awe. And Katya saw Danilo run towards her across that clearing. She rushed to meet him. "Danilushko!"

"Hold on!" The Lady stopped her and turned to Danilo. "Well, Master Danilo, you choose what you want. If you go with her, you'll forget all you've seen here; if you stay — you must forget her and other people."

"I can't forget about other people," he said "And I remember her every single minute."

The Lady smiled kindly and told them "Be it your way, Katerina! Take your man. And because you were so bold and brave, here is a gift from me to you. Let Danilo remember what he's learned here in the mountain. But let him forget this," she waved her hand, and the meadow with those outworldly flowers disappeared. "Go now," she pointed and warned Danilo "Don't tell anyone about the mountain, will ya? Just say you went to a stone master faraway to learn your craft better. And you, Katerina, don't even think I tried to take your groom from you. He came of his own will, but he will forget now why."

Katya gave her a deep bow. "Forgive me, Lady, if I said something wrong."

"Ah," the Lady answered. "I am made of stone, aren't I? Nothing can touch me. Just telling you so you two don't fall out."

Katya and Danilo took a forest path, and it was getting darker and darker as they went, and the ground was uneven, to boot, pits and stones all around. Finally, they looked around and saw that they were at the ore mine, Gumeshki.

It was early so there was nobody about. Little by little they returned home.

***

And those who tried to catch Katya still roamed around shouting to each other "Can you see her yet?" They looked high and low but couldn't find her. And, when they finally came back to the village, they saw Danilo at the window.

They got scared at first, tried to ward him off with some special words and such. And then they saw him prepare his pipe. So they decided he must be alive after all. "A deadman wouldn't smoke a pipe, would he?" they figured.

They began to come closer one by one. And as they did, they saw Katya inside the hut as well, hustling about the pyech and happy. They hadn't seen her like this in a while.

And this is when they gathered their courage to come into the house and ask "Where have you been, Danilo? We haven't seen you in a long time."

"I went to Kolyvan," he said. "I heard there was a stone master over there who had no equals. So I went to learn from him a bit. Father, when he was alive, tried to talk me out of it. But I didn't listen and left in secret. Only Katya knew."

"Why did you break that vase of yours?" they asked.

"Who knows?" he said. "We had a party, right? Mayhap I had one too many. Who knows what I thought? Something I didn't like about it, maybe. Every master breaks what he's made sometimes, eh?"

And then the siblings nagged at Katya some. "Why did you not tell us about Kolyvan?"

But she didn't say much, only noted "The pot calls the kettle black, eh? I did tell you he was alive. And did you listen? No, you tried to talk me into marrying another one and told me I was off my rocker. Just sit at the table already. The food is done."

And so they stopped asking. They stayed a while, talked about this and that and left. In the evening Danilo went to the bailiff to report himself. The bailiff did get angry, of course. But in the end, all was well.

So Katya and Danilo started living in Prokopich's hut. People say they lived well and got along. Danilo was called the Stone Master because of his skill. He was the best master ever, and they had enough money to get by. But once in a while he would get lost in thought.

Katya knew what he was thinking about but said nothing.

The Lady of the Copper Mountain

One day a couple of our guys from the plant went to check the meadows for haymaking. And they had far to go — somewhere beyond Severushka. It was a summer holiday and scorching — as hot as a stove!

The guys were both miners, from the Gumeshki mine. They searched for malachite and ore and found some lasurite too. And, if they found copper crystals or kernels and such, that was alright as well.

One of them was young, unmarried still, but you could see the green in his eyes already — from all that copper dust in the mine, you know. The other one, older, was all worked out. His eyeballs were greenish, and even his cheeks looked moldy. And his cough was telling its tale, for sure.

But it was so good in the forest. Birds sang their cheerful songs, and the earth gave off a light scent like fresh warm dough. And so the guys felt like taking a nap. They reached the Krasnogorka mine, where iron ore used to be mined. They lay on the grass under an ash tree and fell asleep. But then the young one started — as if someone poked him in the side to wake him up.

So he looks up and sees a woman sitting on a pile of ore, near a large stone. She sits with her back to the guy but she has a girl's braid. The braid is black as black and looks so heavy it doesn't move at all. There are ribbons weaved into it, red or green. And those ribbons make a chiming sound like copper sheets would.

The guy wondered at the braid and noticed other things too. The girl was smallish, with pretty curves and so high strung she couldn't sit still. She would bend forward like she was looking for something on the ground, then would sit back or turn to one side or the other. Real intense, that girl.

And she talked fast, but he couldn't make out in what tongue or who she was chatting with. All he heard was she laughed when she spoke. Like she was having fun, she was. He wanted to say something and then halted.

"Oh my, that is the Lady herself! Those are her clothes, for sure. How did I not see that before? I just kept staring at her braid like the fool I am."

And her dress was really one of a kind, made out of silky malachite. There is a stone like this - it looks like real silk and feels like it if you touch it.

"Eh," our guy thought. *"Such misfortune... I need to get away from here before she sees me..."* He heard from the old ones, you see, that this Lady — the Malachite Girl — loves to make fun out of us folks.

And, just as he thought this, she turned around. She looked at our guy, grinning, and told him off merrily "Why are you, Stepan Petrovich, ogling me like this? You look, you buy, eh? Come closer, let's chat."

The guy was afraid, of course, but didn't want to show it. He made a brave face. Even if she is a mystic being, still — a girl. And he, Stepan, is a guy so he cannot be scared of her.

And so he said "I don't have time to chat with you. We have overslept as is. We need to go check on the grass."

She chuckled and then replied "Stop fooling around. Come, I tell ya, I have business for you."

Stepan saw there was nothing to be done. He followed her, as she waved at him and pointed like *"Go around the other way."*

He went around that ore pile like she asked and saw

scores of lizards on the ground — so many and all different. Some were green, others blue as the sky, still others dark blue like deep water — and some were like sand with golden specks. There were lizards that looked like crystalline, and those like old grass, and some with patterns on their tiny backs.

The girl kept on laughing. "Don't step on my army, Stepan Petrovich. Look how big and heavy you are, and they are so little."

And then she clapped, and the lizards moved aside to get out of his way.

Stepan came closer, then stopped. She clapped again and chuckled. "Now you can't go anywhere. If you step on my servants, you'll have bad luck."

He looked at his feet and couldn't see the ground so many lizards were around him. They looked like a multi-patterned moving floor and he saw them for what they might be — different kinds and sorts of copper ore, mica, golden grains. And some lizards looked like real malachite.

"What now, Stepanushko? Do you recognize me?" the Malachite Girl asked, swaying with laughter. And then she added "No need to be afraid. I won't do you any harm."

Stepan felt abashed — no wonder, with a girl mocking him and talking to him like that. He got real peeved so he shouted at her "Why would I be afraid when I mine my hands to the bone in the mountain!"

"There, there," the Malachite Girl said. "You are just what I need — a man who is not afraid of anybody. Tomorrow, when you go down for your shift in the mountain, you'll see your plant's bailiff. So you tell him — and don't forget these exact words — 'the Lady of the Copper Mountain told ya the stinky goat to get well away, out of the Krasnogorka mine. If you keep on meddling with this iron hat of mine, I'll move all Gumeshki's copper down below so you'll never find it in your lifetime."

She said that and squinted at the man. "Did you get it, Stepanushko? You say you work in the mountain and don't fear anyone? So go and tell the bailiff what I asked you to. And don't say anything to the other one who is with you. He is all worked out, won't do any good to mix him up in this business. I've asked the Blue one to help him a bit, too."

She clapped again, and the lizards were all gone. She hopped to her feet as well, climbed on a stone, jumped to another one and, just like a lizard, ran up the mountain in between rocks.

Her arms and legs turned into a lizard's paws, a tail grew, and a black line appeared along her back where her braid used to be. But her head was still a girl's head.

As she reached the top, she turned around and said "Don't forget, Stepanushko, what I said. I told him, the stinky goat, to get the heck away from Krasnogorka. If you do what I ask, I'll marry you."

The guy got so cross he even spat. "Say what? Me, marry a lizard?"

She saw him spit and laughed. "Whatever," she shouted back. "We'll talk afterwards. Maybe you'll change your mind." And she was out of sight, green tail and all.

Stepan was left alone. The mine was all quiet. Only his comrade snored on the other side of the ore pile. Stepan woke him up, and they went to the meadows. They checked the hay grass and returned home towards the evening.

Stepan's mind was heavy. He didn't know what to do. If he said those words to the bailiff, that would be a big deal! And stinky the man was, for real, mayhap something was rotting inside his gut. But if he did not — that would be no good either. She is the Lady, after all. She could change any good ore to nothing. How would he ever mine anything if she did? And, worst of all, he didn't want to look like an empty boast in front of a girl.

He thought and thought and finally found his courage. *"Whatever may be, I'll do what she asks."*

***

Early morning the next day, when the mining folks got together at the mine shuttle to go down, the bailiff came up to them. Everybody took off their hats, of course, and Stepan came closer and said "Last night I saw the Lady of the Copper Mountain and she said to tell you this. She orders you, the stinky goat, to get away from Krasnogorka. If you spoil that iron hat of hers, she will move all Gumeshki's copper down there so that nobody can mine it from below the mountain."

The bailiff's moustache shook with rage. "What? Are you drunk or daft, serf? What lady? How dare you say this to me? You'll rot in the mountain now!"

"Do what you will," Stepan said. "But that's what I was told to say."

"Flog him!" The bailiff screamed. "And then take him to the mine and chain him up down there. Feed him dogs' leftovers so he doesn't kick the bucket and make him mine his due. And, if he doesn't, flog him again till he does."

He got flogged, of course, and they brought him into the mountain. The mine overseer — like the dog he was — put him in the worst stope[7] he could find. It was wet in there, with no good ore to speak of; it should have been abandoned a long time ago. But you know what they did back then when we were bonded? They could do with you whichever way they fancied. They put Stepan on a long

---

[7] A stope is a dugout tunnel or space that contains the ore that is being mined.

chain so that he could work, you see. And the overseer even said "You'll cool off here a bit, and your malachite due is such and such," and he gave a number that was hard to imagine!

But what was there to do? When the overseer left, Stepan took his pickaxe and got to work — he was a nimble miner, ya know. And he looks — it's going well for real. There is so much malachite, like someone throws it at his axe. And the water in the stope is gone, it's warm and dry now. And so he thought "*Ah, the Lady remembers about me, that's good.*"

And, as soon as he thought that, a light shone in the mountain. He saw the Lady right in front of him. And she said "Good job, Stepan Petrovich. You have honored our agreement and didn't fear the Stinky Goat. I heard what you told him and how. Let's go look at my dowry, eh? I keep my word too, I do."

But she frowned like she was not pleased about it. She clapped her hands, the lizards came and freed Stepan from the chain, and the Lady gave them an order. "Mine double his malachite due. And find the best kind, the silk stone."

And then she said to Stepan "Alright, my groom, let's go have a look." And so they went.

She was in the lead, and he followed her. And wherever she turned, the mountain opened. They passed some large rooms with walls of different color. Some were all blue, others yellow with gold specks. Some were covered with copper flowers. And some blue ones were the shade of the sky. Everything was so beautifully decorated it took one's breath away.

And the Lady's dress would change as they went. It would glitter like it was made of crystal, then fade and shine in diamonds — and then change to red copper — and then back to the silk malachite.

After a while, she stopped. "Farther on," she said "There is all yellow and gray stone with speckles — nothing much to look at. But here, we are right under Krasnogorka Mountain. That's my most expensive place after Gumeshki."

Stepan saw a huge room, with all the furniture — beds, tables, stools and chairs — made out of king copper. The walls were malachite with diamond encrustations, and the ceiling was dark-red, black almost, with copper flowers in it.

"Let's sit here and talk," she said.

They sat on those stools and the Lady asked him "Have you seen my dowry?"

"I have," said Stepan.

"So what do you think about marrying me now?"

And Stepan didn't know how to answer her. He had a bride, you see, a good girl and an orphan. She wasn't equal to the Malachite Girl in her beauty, o'course. His sweetheart was just a common human girl. So he got quiet for a bit but then said "Your dowry is good enough for a tzar, and I am a common guy, just a miner."

"My dear friend," the Lady replied "don't beat around the bush. Just tell me, will you marry me or not?" And she frowned even deeper.

Stepan, finally, told her straight "I can't, my Lady. I am betrothed to another one."

He said that and thought *"She's going to get real angry now."* But she seemed glad somehow.

"Good man you are, Stepan," she said. "I commended how you dealt with the bailiff, and commend again how you responded just now. You didn't wish for my riches and didn't choose a stone girl over your Nastyenka." True, his girl's name was Nastya. "Here is a gift for your bride."

And the Lady handed him a big malachite box. "There is everything she might want in that box, women's things — rings, earrings and such that even a rich bride might not have".

"But how," Stepan asked "will I come up from here with a treasure like with?"

"Don't you worry about it. Everything will work out alright. I will help you with the bailiff, and you and your young wife will want for nothing, but remember one thing: don't think about me anymore. This will be your third test."

"And now eat!" She clapped once more, the lizards came and laid the table full of different foods and dishes.

She treated him to a proper borsch, a fish pie, lamb chops, porridge and such — all that would be our custom to serve to a dear guest. And then she said "Farewell now, Stepan Petrovich, mind you not to think about me anymore." But she was crying as she told him that.

She held out her hand and let her tears fall down onto her palm like crystal drops — and gathered a handful of them. "Take these, to help you get started. People will pay big money for these little stones, and you'll be rich." She opened her hand for him to take them.

The stones were cold, but her hand was hot — like she was a living-breathing being — and trembling a little. Stepan took the stones, gave her a deep bow and asked "Where shall I go now?" And glum he was too.

She pointed with her finger, and he saw a way open in front of him, a tunnel that was light like it was daytime.

Stepan followed his way out along that tunnel; he saw the many different wonders again and, finally, went out around his stope. He turned around — and the tunnel closed, and everything looked like it had been before.

A lizard came, put the chain back on his leg, and the malachite box was suddenly so small he could hide it beneath his shirt. Soon the mine overseer arrived. He wanted to mock Stepan, you see, but then saw how much malachite was mined and the quality of the stone, and thought *"How's this? Where did all this malachite come from?"*

He crawled into the stope, looked about and said "Huh, anyone will find good stone in this one." And so he took Stepan to another stope and assigned his nephew to this one.

Next day Stepan got to work again, and there was good malachite flying from under his pickaxe, and even copper crystals or kernels would show; but the overseer's nephew could find nothing, just worthless greystone.

The overseer noticed that and ran to the bailiff. He told the bailiff what had happened and said "The guy must have sold his soul to the devil."

And the bailiff answered "Who cares to whom he sold his soul when we get our profit, eh? Promise him that we will set him free if he finds a malachite slab three hundred stones in weight."

But he did order to unchain Stepan and stop mining works in Krasnogorka.

"Who knows?" he wondered. *"Maybe this fool knew what he was talking about."* Also, the ore they had been mining recently had a lot of copper in it — not good for the cast iron their plant made.

The mine overseer explained to Stepan what they wanted from him, and our guy answered "One would never say no to freedom. I'll do my best — and I will find this slab if luck is with me."

And he did find a slab this large, you know. They dragged it out of the mine — and were very proud of themselves. But they didn't set Stepan free.

They wrote to the barin about the malachite slab, and he came to look at it from Aint-Petersburg itself! He heard the whole story and asked for Stepan.

"Listen here," the barin said. "I give you my noble word that I will set you free if you find malachite stones to make columns out of — no less than thirty-five feet they should be."

Stepan told him "I have been cheated once, I am wise now. Sign the papers to free me first, and then I will mine for those stones — and we'll see if I'm lucky enough to find them."

The barin got all hot under the collar, o'course, stomped his feet, but Stepan stood his ground. "Sign the papers first and — and, also, sign those same papers for my bride too; it won't do if I am free, but she is still bonded."

The barin saw that the guy was tough. He signed the paper to free him. "Here," the barin said. "But do your job well, don't forget!"

And Stepan replied "That's as luck goes."

But, o'course, he found those slabs. He knew the mountain like the fingers on his own right hand, you see, and the Lady helped him too.

They cut columns out of those malachite slabs like they wanted them, dragged them out of the mountain, and the barin sent them to the most important church in Aint-Petersburg. But the first rock that Stepan found is still in our city, they say. It is kept as a rarity, people say.

Stepan was free after that, and Gumeshki got all spent. Lots of lazurite was found, but more of nothing worth mining — no copper, crystal or otherwise, and no malachite whatsoever. And the water in the tunnels began rising.

Gumeshki started to lose profits and then got completely flooded. People say the Lady became upset that her malachite got sent to a church. She doesn't like things like that at all.

***

Stepan didn't live a happy life, in the end. He got married and had kiddies, built a house and his household was all proper. So why not live and be glad? But he was glum all the time, and his health was down and out. He was wasting away fast.

And, sick as he was, he got it into his head to buy a rifle and go hunting. People say he would go to the Kasnogorka mine, but he never came back with any game. And one September morning he left and never came back.

His wife sees he's gone and gone. *"Where would he be?"* she wonders. So our village folks get together and begin looking for him. And they did find him at that mine, lying next to a tall stone.

They see he is dead as dead but with a smile on his pale face, and his rifle lies next to him, and it hasn't been shot once even.

Some people who noticed him first said that there was a green lizard next to the deadman, a huge one like no one had ever seen in our parts. They said it sat next to the man and raised its head when the men approached — and they saw its tears fall onto the corpse. When they came closer, the lizard hopped onto the stone and vanished just like that.

And, when the deadman was brought home and they started washing the body, they noticed his right hand was in a tight fist, but they could see some tiny green grains inside it — a whole handful of those.

One man who knew those things said "This is copper emerald, for sure! A very rare gem, and pricey. You'll be rich, Nastasya, such a fortune they are. But where did he find them, I wonder?"

Nastasya, his wife, said she didn't know anything about that. He did give her a jewelry box when they were still unmarried — a large box made out of malachite and lots of goodies in it — but there was nothing like those little green stones.

And, when folks tried to take those gems out of his dead hand, they turned into dust, so they did. Nobody ever knew how they got to be in his fist to begin with.

People dug around Krasnogorka after that, searching for emeralds. They found nothing but poor copper ore, that was all. Someone started saying later that those were the Lady's tears in Stepan's hand, you see. He never sold them, just kept them in secret all that time — and died holding them in his hand. What do ya know, eh?

That is how it is to meet the Lady of the Copper Mountain!

An ill-natured man will find bad luck, o'course — and a good one will lose his peace of mind.

The Malachite Box

Nastasya, Stepan's widow, still had that malachite box, you know, with all that women's bling: rings and earrings and other pretty things like that. The Lady of the Copper Mountain gifted Stepan with this box when he was getting married.

Nastasya, though, had grown up an orphan and wasn't used to this kind of luxury. Also, she wasn't into donning swanky trinkets. She tried putting on some jewelry from that box, of course, when she and Stepan were just married. But she felt uneasy every single time. She would put on a ring... and it would fit just right — not too tight, not too loose. And then, when she wore it to church or elsewhere, she would always regret it. It would grip her finger like vice so, in the end, the finger would go all blue.

And, if she put some earrings on — even worse — they would hang like lead so her earlobes would swell and hurt. Yet, if she held those earrings in her hand, they were no heavier than her own. As for the six- or seven-line beads, she had only tried them on once. They felt like ice around her neck and would not get any warmer. She never even showed those beads to anybody — out of shame that her neighbors would laugh "Here goes Tzarina of the Polevaya village, all decked out and fancy!"

Stepan, too, never urged her to wear anything from that box. He even said once "Hide it somewhere, better keep it away, to be safe." So Nastasya tucked it in the farthest chest where they kept canvas for clothes and other stuff just in case.

When Stepan died and they found those tiny stones in his dead hand, that's when she finally showed the box to some folks. And that man — the one who had known those tiny stones' value — he said to Nastasya when all the others left "Look here, Nastya, don't sell this box for a trifle. It is worth much money, I say — thousands."

That man, he was educated, and free. He used to be a stone master but got the boot — was too easy on the workers, they said. And he also had a liking for wine. He drank like a fish, not to speak ill of the dead.

Otherwise, he was very much alright. If someone needed something — to write a plea letter, check gold for quality, and other such stuff — he did everything fair and square, not like some who did a half-hearted job just for a bottle. For him, though, everyone was happy to pour a glass or a festive pint. And he lived like so — in our plant's village, fed by the people — till the day he died.

Nastasya had heard from her husband that the stone master was an alright man, and educated, even if he liked his wine a bit much. So she listened to him. "So be it," she said. "I'll keep it for a rainy day," and she put the box back where it belonged.

And thus they buried Stepan, and celebrated the forty days. Nastasya was in her woman's prime, and well-off, so suitors started knocking on her door. But she, being a clever woman, would tell them all the same thing. "Even a golden one, still he'd be a stepfather for the kiddies."

Little by little, they left her alone.

Stepan had provided for his family well enough: a solid house, a horse, all that a family would want for a good life. Nastasya was hard-working, the kids knew discipline, and so they lived and knew no need. But, eventually, they got poor — how can a woman alone with little ones keep things going! And then again, one has to earn a coin or two somehow — if only to buy salt with.

***

Her relatives began their song, nagging her "Sell the box, why don't you? You don't need it, eh? Why waste good stuff? Your daughter Tanyushka — when she grows up — won't wear it anyway. Those tchotchkes are only for the noble ones, the rich ones. Who would wear them with our rags? And some rich folks would give you money — good help for your housekeeping."

So you see, they tried to talk her into it, by hook or by crook. And the buyers — like ravens to the bones — landed on her porch in flocks. They were merchants, mainly. One would buy it for one hundred rubles, another one was ready to give two hundred. "We feel for your littles ones," they said, "driving a good bargain for you, the widow," they said.

They wanted to make a fool of her, you see, but she was not that kind of bird.

Nastasya minded well that the old mining master told her not to sell that box for a trifle. And a pity it would be to sell it, too — her groom's wedding gift and her dead husband's memory. Moreover, her youngest, Tanyushka, would burst into tears and plead "Dear mommy, please don't sell it. Better if I go look for a servant's work than lose Daddy's keepsake."

Stepan, you see, left three little ones behind. There were two lads and this littlest one — the odd one — who did not look like the mother or the father. Even when Stepan was still alive and she was teeny-tiny, all the folks wondered at her.

Be it women or men, everybody told him "It's like you made this one in your workshop, Stepan. Who does she take after, so pretty, with that black hair of hers and those green eyes? Doesn't look like any other girls in the village."

And Stepan would joke back. "No wonder her hair is black when her daddy has played underground since he was little. And the green eyes? No wonder either. You know how much malachite I have worked for Barin Turchaninov

— got myself a little keepsake too." He even called his girl Keepsake. "Hey you, my little Keepsake." And, when he could buy something for her, he would always bring something blue or something green.

This little girl grew, and people would take notice of her. And so pretty was she, like a bead fell out of a fancy gown — seen from afar. And though she didn't care much for people's love, everybody still called her "Tanyushka, Tanyushka!"

Even the most envious folks took joy in looking at her. "Such a beauty!" Only her mother sighed "Beautiful she is for sure, but not ours. It's like she is someone else's child."

This girl, she took Stepan's death hard, very hard. She cried night and day, got all thin and pale in the face, only eyes left. So Nastasya thought to give her the malachite box. *"Let her play with it,"* she thought. "*Any girl — even if a kid still — loves pretty things like that."*

Tanyushka got to sort through the stuff that was in the box. And — whatever she tries on — a green-eyed wonder — everything fits! Nastasya didn't even know how to wear some of those trinkets — and the girl sees how to put on what. And she kept on saying "Mommy, Daddy's gifts are so good, it's like you sit in the sun and someone nice and warm strokes your back."

Nastasya couldn't stop wondering. She remembered how her fingers got all blue, her ears would swell and her neck felt like she was wearing ice. And she thought *"Ah, something is up with that box; something really odd is up."* So she hid the box back into the chest.

But ever since Tanyushka would pester her now and then. "Mommy, Mommy, let me play with the Daddy's gift, please." Nastasya would scold her a bit, but her mother's heart would soften up, and she would fetch the box for her, saying "Don't you break anything!"

Later, when Tanyushka grew up a bit, she would take the box out herself too. When Nastasya and the boys made for the fields for haymaking, they would leave the girl to keep the house. She would, of course, first do what her mother told her — wash up, sweep the floors, feed the chicks, see if the pyech needed minding.

She would finish things up as fast as she could — and go get the box out of that bottom chest. They didn't have many chests left by then, and the one above was very light. So she would move that upper one aside, take the box out, open it and gaze at the stones, trying on this thing and that.

One time a burglar got into the house. No one knew if he had sneaked in in the wee hours and lay low till everyone had gone out, or climbed over the fence while nobody was looking. The neighbors said they didn't see anyone. A stranger he was, but somebody must've tipped him off, you see, told him about the box and stuff.

Once Nastasya left, Tanyushka ran around doing the housekeeping and such, and, afterwards, she quieted down to play with the father's stones. She had put on the headpiece and hung the earrings — and that's when that bad man rushed into the hut.

Tanyushka looked and saw a stranger in the doorway, with an axe — and the axe of their own, the one that had stood in the corner at the entrance door. She had just moved it to the side when she swept the floor in the mudroom.

Tanyushka got fearful, for sure, but the man saw her and shrieked. He dropped the axe, clapped his eyes like something burned them and started moaning "Oh my, I am blind, my eyes, I am blind" and rubbing his eyes.

Tanyushka saw something was wrong with the man and asked "Who are you, uncle[8]? How did you get in and why did you take our axe?"

But he — whatever she said — just moaned and rubbed his eyes some more. Tanyushka felt sorry for the guy and filled a ladle with water. But, when she wanted to give it to him, he stumbled back like it was boiling hot.

"Don't you come near me!" he yelled. He backed away into the mudroom and put something up against the door so she couldn't jump out at him.

But she found another way out — she got out of the window and ran to the neighbors. The neighbors came running. They asked him who he was and what he was doing at Nastasya's home.

Blinking, he explained that he, a beggar, wanted to ask for some food or such — but something happened to his eyes. "Like the sun itself. I thought — that's it; I've gone blind. Maybe it's the heat that caused it."

And Tanyushka did not say a word about the axe and her Daddy's gemstones. So they thought *"Ah, no big deal, maybe she herself forgot to lock the gate, so he came in and then felt unwell for some reason or other. Stuff happens."*

Still, they didn't let the vagabond go before Nastasya returned. And then, when she came back, the man told her the same thing he said to the neighbors. Nastasya saw that everything was in its proper place and decided not to raise alarms. So he left, and the neighbors too.

***

Only then Tanyuska told her mother how it really happened. And Nastasya made out that the vagabond

---

[8] In Russia, adults used to be called "uncle" and "auntie", even if they were strangers.

really came for the jewelry box, but it wasn't so easy to take, it turned out. She thought to herself *"We do need to keep it safe for certain."* And she took it in secret, dug a hole in the basement and hid the box like that.

Next time, when all the family left, Tanyushka couldn't find the box anywhere. She was about to start crying when she felt warm all of the sudden. *"Where is that coming from? What the heck?"*

So she looked around and saw some light coming from under the floorboards. *"Is the house on fire?"* she thought, startled. She even got a bucket with water, but, when she got close, she saw there was no fire or smoke at all.

Tanyshka started digging where the light was — and here was her box. She opened it and the stones looked even prettier than before, all sparkles and sunlight. She didn't even take the box up into the house. She just played with it in the basement as long as she felt like.

And so it started. The mother thinks *"Ah, I hid it well, nobody knows."* And the daughter, when everyone's away and she's done housekeeping, plays with Daddy's gifts to her heart's desire.

Also, Nastasya didn't even listen when her folks told her to sell the box. "When it comes to beggaring — then I'll sell it, but not before."

Living wasn't easy, but, still, Nastasya toughed it out. They did live from hand to mouth for some years, but then things started turning up. The older boys began bringing a bit of money home, and Tanyushka didn't sit still. She, you know, learned embroidery on silk. And she got so good at it that even barin's seamstresses would stare in awe. "Where did she take those patterns from, and the beads and silk?" they said.

And then another thing happened. A woman came by their house, a small one, in Nastasya's years, with black hair and sharp eyes, and oh, so sly, you had to keep your eyes open. All she had was a canvas rucksack and a cherrywood staff in her hand — like a pilgrim or such. And so she asked Nastasya "May I rest at your hearth for a while? My road is long, and my legs won't carry me."

Nastasya thought a bit — maybe another one was sent after the box — but decided to let her in, in the end. "Space we have, and you are welcome to share it. Our food, though, is but an orphan's meal. There's onions with kvas[9] in the morning, and kvas with onions at night — all the change there is. If you aren't afraid of our skinny diet, come on in and live as long as you want."

But the pilgrim woman had already set her wooden staff by the stove and taken her boots off. Nastasya didn't care much for this but said nothing. *"What manners, eh? Hardly had I said welcome, and she feels like she is at home already — taking off boots and setting her bags where she wants."*

And the woman, meanwhile, undid her backpack and beckoned Tanyushka with her finger. "Come, child of mine, look at my needlework. If you are keen, I'll teach you the trade. Your eyes are sharp, I see."

Tanhyshka came up to her, and the woman showed her a band with silk embroidery on the ends. And, you see, the pattern on it was so hot — like it suddenly got warmer and lighter in the hut, ya know. Tanyushka is all eyes, and the woman chuckles "Ah, so you do like my work, do you? Want me to show how it's done?"

"Yes!" said the girl. "Teach me. Please."

Nastasya snapped when she heard that. "Don't even think about it. We have no spare money to buy salt with, what of silk needlework! The materials must cost a fortune, don't they!"

---

[9] A fermented drink, similar to kombucha

"Don't worry about this, my kind hostess," the woman said. "When your girl learns the craft, she'll have all the materials she needs. I'll leave some to her for your hospitality. And then you'll see for yourself. We are paid well for our skill, you know. We don't work for nothing and earn our breadworth."

Nastasya gave in after these words. "If you give her stuff to work with, why not? Let her study if she has a knack for it. I will be grateful to you for that."

So this woman began to teach Tanyushka. The girl got the hang of the skill fast — like she had known it before from somewhere. And, what's more, Tanyushka didn't show much love to anyone, be it neighbors or her own mother. Yet, she would cling to the pilgrim woman like a puppy. Nastasya looked askance. *"Found herself a new mother, did she? Never gives me a hug, but she is all over this tramp."*

And the woman — as if to tease Nastasya — would call the girl "my sweet child", "daughter of mine" and such — and never mentioned her Christian name, not once. Tanyushka saw her mother's resentment but could not help herself.

She trusted the woman so much that she even told her the secret about that box they had. "We have my dad's gift to remember him by — a box made of malachite. Such amazing stones, I could look and look at them for hours."

"Will you show me, my child?" the woman asked. And Tanyushka didn't think twice about it. "I will," she said. "When everybody's gone out".

When the chance came, she asked the woman to come down to the cellar with her. She took out the box, opened it and the woman said "Put them on, will you? I will see them better that way."

And Tanyushka started to put the stone jewelry on at once, while the woman kept saying how good she looked. "Such pretty stones, my child, real pretty. Just let me straighten this one up right here." The woman came closer and began to touch the stones here and there. And whichever stone she touched would shine anew and different. Tanyuska saw some of what happened, but not all.

By and by, the woman said "Stand straight, child of mine, will you?" The girl did as she was told while the woman kept stroking her hair and her back. And then she told Tanyuska "When I ask you to turn, you do that but don't look at me. Look in front of you and see what is to come but say nothing. Now, turn!"

Tanyushka did, and saw a room like she had never seen in her life — maybe a church, or some other fancy place. The ceilings were high, held up by the columns of pure malachite. The walls were also done in malachite as tall as a man's height, and the upper eaves were laid in a complex malachite pattern.

And so she sees a beautiful lady in front of her standing like in a mirror, and she is so pretty like they tell in fairytales, with hair like night and shining green eyes. She is wearing precious stones and a velvet dress, green but playing with other colors in the bright light. And her dress is cut like those of tzarinas and queens in paintings — with the cut so deep you wouldn't know how it doesn't fall away. Our factory girls would be too ashamed to wear something like this, but this one, with the green eyes, is standing calm, like everything is as it is supposed to be.

And that room is crowded with folks dressed like nobles, some clothes are embroidered with gold while others wear shoulder straps and medals — some of that fancy stuff is at the front of their jackets, some on their backs; others are all covered in those tricks and trifles.

So they all look like the most important barins, you see. And their wives are all bare-armed and bare-breasted, with all kinds of precious stones on them. But they can't compare to the green-eyed girl — not a single one would come close in beauty.

And there is some fair-haired guy standing next to the green-eyed lady. He is cross-eyed, and his ears stick out like a hare's. And his clothes are so bizarre — like he didn't think golden threads and tricks would be enough, he even put some stones on his boots, you see. And such rare stones they are — you might find one of those maybe once in a dozen years. So one could see immediately — he is a factory or plant owner, you know. And so he blabbers something, but she looks like he is not there at all.

Tanyushka stared at the green-eyed lady and finally saw that the gems she had on were her Dad's gift, from their malachite box.

"Ah!" she said. "Those are ours!" And it all just vanished.

And the vagabond woman chuckled "You didn't finish watching, my dear child. Oh well, you'll get another chance when time comes."

And Tanyushka got curious, of course, and asked "Where is this fancy place?"

And so the woman told her. "This," she said "is the Tzar's palace. This is the room which is done in malachite over there. Your dead father mined that malachite, you know."

"And who is the one wearing my Daddy's stones — and that hare of a man, who is he?"

"Can't tell you, sweet child of mine. You'll soon find out for yourself."

***

That same day, when Nastasya returned home, the woman began getting ready to leave. She bowed deeply to the hostess, gave Tanyushka a bundle with silks and beads and then took out a tiny button from her pocket — glass or some cheap stone it was, who knows.

She handed it over to Tanyshka and said "Take this, my sweet child, to remember me by. If you get stymied during your needwork, or have some hard choice to make, just look at it; you'll think of a way to go about it."

She said that and left. And nobody saw her since.

By then Tanyshka got real skilled at needlework and embroidery. At that time she was already coming of age and looked lovely. The plant guys would ogle her but never came close. She was cold and glum, that one, not to mess with — and why would a free one marry a bondsman, with a yoke around his neck?

The barin's folks heard about Tanyushka's craftsmanship. And they started sending some young guys to lure her in. They would dress a lackey in a rich man's clothes, give him a watch on a chain and send him to Tanyushka's — like he is there on some business — thinking *"Mayhap she will fall for one of those and we would take her in, as a house seamstress."*

But nothing came out of that. Tanyushka would be all business and would not pay any mind to any other talk. And if the guy kept annoying her, she would make a fool out of him with her jokes. "You go now, dear man, go, I tell ya. They are waiting for you at the barin's house, eh? Don't they fear your watch will stop and the chain will go dull — I see how you worry it in your hard-worked fingers."

So the lackey or other servant who was sent would run off like a scalded dog. "That is not a girl, that one! Just a green-eyed statue made of stone! I'll find a better one."

And so he grumbles, but he's head over heels already. Whoever they sent couldn't forget Tanyushka's beauty. They would come back, as if mesmerized, to catch a glimpse of her, even just through a window, for a little bit. On holidays all bachelors would take walks past that window. A path appeared where there was none, but Tanyushka would not look at any of them.

The neighbors got to telling Nastasya off. "Why is your Tanyushka such a high-brow? No friends she has, and no beau. Is she waiting for a prince to come and fetch her or will she be a Christ's bride, this one?"

Nastasya listened to them and sighed. "I don't know, my dear ones. She was never easy, but after that vagabond witch I can't get to her at all. If I tell her something, she'll just stare at the witch's button and say nothing back. I would throw this button in the river but it does help her in her needlework. If she thinks how to change the silk or the thread pattern, she'll just look at the button. She showed me, too, but my eyes are no good anymore, I can't see much. I would spank her, but she is our breadwinner, you see. We mostly live on what she gets for her craft. And so I think like that and cry sometimes. And then she says 'Mommie dear, I know that my fate is not here. That is why I don't get close to anyone and don't join games like others. Why would I make people sad on purpose? And, if I sit at the window, this can't be helped. I need light for work, you know that. Why do you scold me? Have I done anything wrong?' And what can I say to that, eh?"

Their living improved, o'course. Tanyushka's craft was in fashion. Not only our plant folks and city folks knew about it, but she even got orders from other places, and solid money it was. A good man would earn as much.

But just then a bad thing happened. There was a fire in the middle of the night. Their barn, the horse, all their cattle

— all was gone in that fire. They only had what was on their backs when they ran out. Nastasya saved the malachite box, though. The following day she said "We do have to sell the box now."

And her sons agreed in one voice. "Just don't sell it for a trifle, remember?"

Tanyshka stole a glance at her button and saw the green-eyed one wave her hand — like *let them sell it, don't you worry*. She was bitter, o'course, but she knew that the jewelry from that box would go to Green Eyes anyway. So she sighed and said "Alright, sell it if you must."

And she didn't even take a last look at the stones. And then again, they were spending the night at the neighbor's house, no sense to take everything out and show it to anyone.

So they made up their mind to sell it. And, no sooner they had, merchants came from all places — those who knew the value of good things and could wait. One of them might even have started that fire, eh?

They saw that the kids had grown up some and were ready to buy it for more now — five hundred, seven hundred. One of them offered a thousand even. For those who work in the plant that is good money — you can get a new household for that. But Nastasya still decided to ask for two thousand. And so they came, those rascals, and tried to get a good bargain for themselves without telling one another. The morsel was so good they didn't want to lose it.

***

Meanwhile, a new bailiff arrived in Polyevaya.

Usually bailiffs don't change too often, but something must've come up. The Stinky Goat, the one that was the bailiff in Stepan's days — he got sent away by the old barin, so smelly he was. Then we had the Roasted Ass — the one that the workers put on the hot stove. After him there was Severyan the Slaughterer, and the Lady of the Mountain took care of that one. And there were two or three others, but then this new one came.

They say he was from some faraway land, and spoke different languages, but his Russian was not too good. And the only word he was good at was "Flog him!" And he would say it like singing "Flahhg — heeem!" Whatever wrong happens — "Flahhg—heem!" he screams. And so we called that one "Flahgim".

To be fair, Flahgim was not too bad. He would scream and shout but did not really send too many to the floggers. The floggers, they didn't have much to do in Flahgim's days, and the folks got a bit of relief.

The thing is, the old barin became real frail by that time, and could hardly walk. So he made it up to marry his son to some Dutchess or such. But the young barin had a mistress, you see, and he was very fond of her. What to do? Things were a bit awkward. What would the new matchmaker say?

That was why the old barin decided to talk the mistress-lady into marrying a musician. That musician was part of the barin's estate. He would teach the little barins some music and some foreign tongues as was custom.

"Instead of living like you do, why don't you get married and clear your name from all gossip. I'll give you a proper dowry and assign your husband as Polevaya's bailiff. Business is going well there, he just needs to keep it tight. I reckon even a musician will have enough mind for that. You will have a good living there, in Polevaya — you'll be the most important person there, and everyone will give you love and respect. How's that?"

The woman understood what's what. Maybe she was upset with the young barin for something or had some back thoughts. Anyway, she agreed. "I have wanted that for a long time now," she said. "But I wouldn't dare say."

Well, the musician was unwilling at first. "Don't want her, she has a bad name, that one. They call her a whore."

But the old barin was sly — he did build that estate with his smarts, ya know — so he knew ways to change the foreigner's mind. Maybe he threatened the guy — or promised him something in return — or just got him drunk enough — whatever he did, the wedding soon took place, and the newlyweds were sent off to Polevaya.

That is how we got to have Flahgim at our plant. He did not last long — but no speaking ill of the dead. And then, when the Double Face took his place, our folks even remembered that Flahgim with a good word.

***

Flahgim and his wife arrived around the time when the merchants walked circles around Nastasya. The wife was a good-looking woman, with white skin and rosy cheeks — a pretty one. And then again, the young barin wouldn't have taken an ugly one, eh?

And so this Flahgim's wife heard stories about the malachite box and thought "Huh! Why don't I go look — mayhap it's something valuable for real." And she got dressed and ready and headed for Nastasya's. The barin's folk, they always have horses ready so why not?

"Well," the barinya said when she arrived. "Dear woman, show me those gems I've heard about, will ya?"

Nastasya got the box out and opened it to show what was inside. The wife's eyes got all wide and bright, o'course. She grew up in the actual Aint-Peterburg and went around to foreign counties and such. So she knew the value of jewelry like that. *"How come?"* she thought.

"The Tzarina herself does not own such beauty, and here, in Polevaya, a peasant woman ... Just need to make sure I secure this buy."

"How much do you want for that?" she asked Nastasya.

"Two thousand rubles," Nastasya answered.

"I don't have this kind of money on me". Flahgim's wife said. "Why don't you come with me to my place? I'll give you your money there."

But Nastasya did not give in to this one. "It is not our custom here for the bread to run after the mouth. Go bring the money — and the box is yours."

The barinya sees how Nastasya is and tells her "I'll be right back. Don't sell it to anyone before I return, eh?"

Nastasya says "That for sure, my lady. I keep my promises. I'll wait for you till the evening, and, if you don't come, I'll do as I like."

Flahgim's wife went off, and the merchants ran into the house at once. They had kept watch, you see. "So," they asked. "What did the lady say?"

"She is buying the box," Nastasya answered.

"For how much?"

"Two thousand, like I asked."

"Have you lost your mind, woman?" the merchants cried. "Giving it off into strange hands — why don't you sell it to us for more?" They began to up the price but Nastasya did not take the bait.

"It's you," she said "you're the ones who don't keep your word when the profit is good. I am not like that. I told the woman I'll keep it for her, and that's that."

Flahgim's wife came back fast. She handed Nastasya the money, fetched the box and was about to head home. And, as she turned to leave, she ran into Tanyushka in the doorway. Tanyshka, you see, had stepped out for some errands or such, so the sell took place without her.

Tanyushka sees a barinya with her malachite box — but not the one she saw in her vision back then. And so she stares at the lady — and Flahgim's wife stares back.

"Who are you, girl? Where do you come from?"

Nastasya says "Folks call her my daughter — the rightful heir to that box you bought. Wouldn't have sold it if the need wasn't so bad. My daughter has played with those stones since she was a little one, you know. She would enjoy how warm and shiny those trifles were. But what's the point? What's gone is gone."

"Don't say that, my sweet woman." said Flahgim's wife. "I will find good use for those stones." And she thought to herself *"This Green Eyes can't know how much power she has. If she were in Aint-Petersburg, she would have tzars wrapped about her little finger. My fool Turchaninov must not see her".*

And then she left.

***

When she got back home, Flahgim's wife wanted to show off her new jewelry. "Look, hubbie," she said. "With such a treasure I don't need either you or Turchaninov. Au revoir — whenever I feel like it! I can go to Aint-Petersburg or — even better — travel abroad, sell that box over there and buy husbands like you by the dozen if I want."

So she boasted and ran off to the mirror, to try on the new trifles. A woman, sure! She put on the headpiece first. *"Ouch! Ouch! What is that?"* It gripped her head like a vice and her hair got tangled in it. She had to tear it away together with some hair roots. And still, she couldn't wait to try on something else. She donned the earrings — but they almost ripped her ears off. And her finger got all blue when she put on a ring. She had to lather it with soap to pull it off. Her husband, meanwhile, chuckled to himself. "Not for the likes of you such things were made."

Finally, she thought of something. *"Ah, I need to go to town and find a master for a better fit. He'll fix everything — I just need to make sure he doesn't swap the stones".*

She went the following morning, like she decided. When you have the plant's troika[10], nothing is too far, eh?

She asked about the most reliable stone master and dropped by the workshop. The master was very old but the best in his craft. He looked over the box and asked her where she got it from. She told him what she knew. He gave the box one more look, but didn't even look inside.

"Not gonna take it," he said. "No matter how much you will give. This work is not from here; the masters who made it are not our equals, and that's that."

The barinya did not get why he said what he said — she just snorted and ran off to other masters. But all of them did the same thing: examined the box, marveled at the craftsmanship without even opening the lid and said a hard no.

The barinya tried to be coy about it and said she brought the box from Aint-Petersburg — that's where all that jewelry and the box itself came from. But the master she told it to just laughed at her. "Say no more," he said. "For I know where this box comes from and heard about the master a lot. None of ours are a match to his mastery. Whatever we do, this jewelry was fitted by him for only one person, and only that person can wear it. Can't be helped, I tell ya."

The barinya did not understand everything but one thing she saw — strange was that box and the masters were fearful. And she recalled how Nastasya told her that her daughter loved trying on those stones.

"Mayhap, that jewelry was fitted for Green Eyes. Such a shame!"

---

[10] A troika was a carriage drawn by three horses.

And then she figured *"Ah, never mind, I can sell the box to some rich fool, and be done with it. Let her fiddle with these tricks, and I'll have the money anyway."* And, thinking that, she went to Polevaya.

***

Once she got there, she heard that the old barin had kicked the bucket. Sly was he when he made her marry Flahgim, but death got to be slyer — it just came and snuffed him out.

He had had a plan to marry his son to a noble one, but did not carry it out. And now the young barin was the lord and owner of all the estate. Flahgim's wife got a letter from him in a little while. "Dear love," he wrote. "I'll arrive to check on the plant when the river runs full. I'll get you rid of that musician somehow and take you back for myself."

Flahgim heard about it from somewhere and flew off the handle. No fun it is when you get robbed of your wife in public, eh? So he turned to the bottle, with his underlings, of course. And what of that? Everybody's happy when drinks are free.

And so, one day, while they were belting down, one of them boasted "Such a beauty we have at our plant village — you won't find any like her in the whole world." Flahgim asked who that was and where she lived. They told him and mentioned the box "That is where your wife got it from, you see."

Flahgim got into his head "I want to see her!" and the drunkards had an idea how to go about that.

"We can go right now," they said "like we want to check how they are faring in their new hut. They are free men but live on the plant land. We can pretend we are there to see, mayhap they used too much land to build their hut on."

There were two of them who went — three if you count Flahgim. They brought a chain with them and got to measuring the plot — as if to make sure all is properly done — fault-finding, ya know.

Then they came into the hut, and Tanyushka was home alone at that time. Flahgim had one look at her and swallowed his tongue. He never saw any woman more beautiful than this village girl was.

So he stood like a fool he was, and she sat like there was no one gawking at her.

Finally Flahgim got to his senses somewhat and asked her "What is it you're doing, dear girl?"

"It's embroidery some folks ordered," she said and showed him her work.

"Can I give you an order?" he asked her.

"Why not? If the price is right."

"Can you make a portrait of yourself on silk for me?"

Tanyushka glanced at her button — and the green-eyed woman inside it waved at her — *sure, take the order* — and pointed at herself. Tanyuska told him "Can't make my own portrait, but I know a woman who will be a good model, in her Tzarina dress and malachite jewelry. But such work doesn't come cheap."

"No doubt about that," he said. "I can pay you two hundred rubles — but only if she looks like you."

"She will look like me," Tanyushka said "but in a different dress."

She asked for one hundred rubles for that portrait. She gave him a time to come back for his order — one month. But he would run by every once in a while before the deadline — like he needed to ask her about their business. He was charmed by her — head over heels — and Tanyushka makes like she doesn't know it. She'll say two or three words to him, and that's it. His drunkard buddies started to make fun of him a bit. "That's all in vain, don't you know. She's not going to even look at you twice."

Tanyushka finished the silk portrait. Flahgim looked at it in awe — the portrait was Tanyushka herself, but wearing those wonderful stones and a rich dress. And he gave her three hundred — but she only took one.

"It is not our custom to take gifts," she said "We live on what we have earned."

Flahgim ran back home with that portrait. He couldn't stop staring at it in wonder but kept it hidden from his wife. He started drinking less, and cared more about what went on at the plant.

***

The young barin came for a visit in spring. He took his troika carriage to Polevaya. The villagers were sent out in the streets to greet him, the priest served a mass and then the dancing and drinking began. Us common folks were given two barrels of wine — to remember the old barin by and to cheer for the young one.

Such a treat that was, and then the folks would spend the last of their money to chase that first cup. But they remembered that barin poured the first one and praised him, you see. The Turchaninovs were clever masters. The next day common folks would have to go back to work, and the barins would go on partying.

And so it went on like that for a few days. The barin's folks would party, sleep, then drink some more. They went on boat rides and took their horses to the woods, there would be music and what not. Flahgim would drink like a fish all those days. The barin, you see, sent some people to pour him so he would drink till he was dead. And those folks were happy to make up to the young master.

Meanwhile, the drunk Flahgim still saw where things were going. He felt bad that everyone knew his wife slept with the barin, you see. So he said one day in front of all that party "I don't care that the barin wants to take my wife from me. Let him do what he likes. I don't need her when I have this one."

And he showed the silk portrait he had in his pocket. Everyone just sighed in amazement, and his wife's jaw dropped. And the barin, you see, gawked at the portrait mesmerized like.

"Who is that? he asked.

Flahgim laughed like crazy and said "Won't tell ya even if you give me a chest of gold."

But what's the point? The folks from the plant knew exactly who that woman was and told the barin.

Flahgim's wife waved her hands at them. "What nonsense, you people! Where would a village girl find a dress like this and such gems? My husband bought this portrait when we traveled abroad. I saw it long before we wed. Drunk y'all are, that's it. You don't know what y'all are saying."

Flahgim saw that his wife was real miffed, and he went on "Shame on you, you shrew! What tales you weave, when did I show you that portrait? It was made for me here, by the very same girl the folks talk about. Don't know anything about her dress. The dress is mayhap made up, but she used to have those gemstones — the same stones you hide now in your wardrobe. You yourself bought them for two thousand rubles, but are not fit to wear. Cows aren't meant to wear saddles, eh? All the plant knows about your buy."

When the barin heard about the gems, he was like "I want to see them now!"

He was not the sharpest tool in the shed, that one, keen on throwing money around — well, he was the heir so he could. And he was especially fond of gems and stones, you know. He didn't have much to recommend him — not by height or by voice — so he did his best to show off his clothes and jewels. As soon as he heard about a good one, he would rush there to buy it.

Flahgim's wife saw that nothing could be done and brought out the box. Once the barin had a good look, he wanted to buy everything at once. "How much?" he demanded.

She asked for some crazy money. He got to bargaining about it. Finally, they agreed on the half, and the barin signed an I-O-U paper — he didn't have this much money on him, o'course. When that was settled, the barin put that box on the table in front of him, and said "I want to see that girl y'all been talking about."

Tanyushka was sent for. She came; she thought there was maybe a big order coming her way.

So she comes into the room — and it's all crowded — and she sees that very hare of a man she saw in her vision. He has her father's box in front of him, her Daddy's gift.

Tanyushka recognized him at once and said "Why did you want to see me, my lord?"

And the barin looks like the cat got his tongue, you see — just stares at her and that's that.

In the end, though, he got himself together and asked her. "Are those gems yours?"

"They were," she answered. "But they're theirs now." And she pointed to Flahgim's wife.

"They are mine already," the young barin boasted.

"It's none of my business whose they are, " she said.

"I can give them back to you if you want."

"There is nothing I can give you in return." she replied.

"Can you at least try them on?" the barin said. "I want to see what they will look like on a living woman."

"That," Tanyushka said "I can do."

She opened the box, took out what she wanted and put everything on where it belonged. And the barin only gawked at her and sighed — "oh" and "woah" and no other words.

Tanyshka stood a bit with those gems on, and then said "Is that enough now? I don't have time to stand around here all day — I've got work to do."

And the barin says in front of all folks just like that "Marry me! Will ya?"

She just chuckled and said "Why would a barin say something like that to a common girl?" She took off the jewelry and left.

But the barin wouldn't give up. He came to Nastasya the next day and begged her to give him Tanyushka for a wife.

Nastasya told him "She is a free woman and she can marry you if she wills — but I don't think you are the right fit."

Tanyushka listened to this and said "I have heard that there is a special room in the Tzar's palace decorated with the malachite that my father mined. If you show me the Tzarina in that room, I'll marry you."

The barin, of course, agreed to whatever she wanted. He started getting ready to go to Aint-Petersburg and told her "Come with me, I'll give you a troika." But she answered "It is not our custom for the bride to arrive at the wedding on her groom's horses, and we are not even that. We'll talk about it after you keep your promise."

"So when," he asked "will you arrive in Aint-Petersburg?"

"I will be there by Virgin of Mercy's[11]," she said "You'll see me then. You can go now."

The barin left, having forgotten about Flahgim's wife. When he came to Aint-Petersburg, he got to boasting about the gemstones and his bride. He showed the box to

---

[11] A religious holiday celebrated by the Orthodox church in the middle of October.

many folks. And everybody was curious to see the new girl.

By the fall, the barin found an apartment for Tanyushka, bought her lots of dresses and shoes and such, and then he received a letter from her telling him she was already in town and staying at a widow's place, on the outskirts.

He went there at once and tried to talk her into moving out. "The apartment is ready," he said "First-rate accommodation. How can you even stay here in a poor woman's house like this?"

But she answered "I feel comfortable here. I'm staying."

Even the Tzarina heard about the jewelry box and the beauty of Turchaninov's bride. So the Tzarina said "I wish to see Turchaninov's bride. Too much gossip around her."

The barin visited Tanyushka again. He told her she needed a dress to go to the palace and reminded her to put the gems on. Tanyushka told him "Don't you worry about what I will wear, but you are right about the stones. I'll take them for the time being. And don't even think about sending horses to get me. I will get there on my own. Just you wait for me at the entrance, on the porch."

The barin thought "Where will she find a dress good enough to go to the palace? And the horses?" but did not dare ask.

***

They had a ball at the palace. Everybody came in beautiful carriages and dressed in silks and velvet. Barin Turchaninov hung about the palace porch since early morning, looking out for his bride. Other people were curious and wanted to see her too.

Tanyushka, though, put on the jewels, got her old plant coat on and a kerchief around her head — like she would wear in her village.

And so she walks towards the palace, with no rush whatsoever. All the folks follow her — strange is this one, where is she from?

She came up to the palace, but the servants wouldn't let her in. "This place is not for workers or village girls like you," they said. Turchaninov saw Tanyushka from afar, but felt ashamed that his bride arrived on foot and in a coat like this, so he hid behind a column.

Tanyushka, though, undid her old fur coat, and the servants saw the dress beneath it — such a dress it was that even a tzarina would envy. Tanyushka took off the kerchief and the coat, and everybody sighed and murmured "Where is this tzarina from? Which foreign lands?"

Turchaninov appeared next to her at once. "This is my bride," he said. Tanyushka looked at him coldly "We'll see about that! Why didn't you wait for me at the gate like I told ya?"

The barin tried to talk his way out of this but... Anyways, he apologized and they went into the palace, where they were told to.

Tanyushka looked around and told Turchaninov even colder than before "This is not the place I told you to take me. Why don't you keep your promise? I told you to take me to the room which was made out of malachite that my daddy mined." And she went around the palace like she was at home there. And all the senators and generals just tagged along. They thought *"If she goes to a different room, that's where everybody has been told to go."*

So she found that Malachite Room, you see. And it got all crowded, with all those folks who followed her to the room. They all look at her, and she just stands at the malachite wall, waiting calmly. Turchaninov runs around her, blabbering that this is not the spot where the Tzarina told them to wait. But she acts like he is not there at all — doesn't even turn her head his way.

The Tzarina came to the room where everybody was told to wait for her and saw no one. A servant whispered to her that Turchaninov's bride had led everyone into the Malachite Room.

The Tzarina grumbled a bit and stomped her feet. "How dare anyone disobey in the Tzar palace!" She got all flushed, you know. But, in the end, she went to the Malachite Room as well. Everybody bowed to her, but Tanyushka stood straight.

The Tzarina commanded in a loud voice "Where is that woman who doesn't know our rules? Show me that bride of yours, Turchaninov!"

When Tanyushka heard these words, she raised a brow and said to the barin "Is that what is going on? You promised to show me the Tzarina, but it is the other way around! I am being shown to her, eh? Liar! Don't want to see you anymore. Take your stones!"

And as she said this, she leaned against the malachite wall and melted into it. The only thing left was the gemstones. They were hanging in the places where her head, neck and hands used to be.

Everybody got scared, of course, and the Tzarina fainted and dropped to the floor. People started to hustle about her, to get her back on her feet. And then, when things calmed down a bit, some folks told Turnachinov "Go pick up those gems fast — someone will steal them if you don't. We are in a palace, after all. People know the value of those here."

Barin Turchaninov tried to pick up those stones, o'course. But each one he touched would turn into a drop. Some drops were clear like tears, others — yellow, another one would be like blood, thick and red. So he never recovered any of them.

And then he spotted a glass button — like bottle glass, with a simple cut — no value to it, he saw. But he still picked it up, in a bitter mood. And when he looked into that button, he saw the green-eyed beauty in the malachite dress, wearing those stones he lost. And she laughs and laughs at him "You stupid crossed-eyed hare! How could you think you could have me as your bride?"

The barin — feeble in the head as he was — lost his mind completely after that. But he didn't throw away that button, you see. He would look at it and at Green Eyes laughing at him inside it.

Bitter he became, and took to the bottle because of that. He wasted away all his fortune like that and made a lot of debts so our plants almost closed down!

Flahgim was fired too, and he went to the pubs. He drank till he had nothing but the clothes on his back, but wouldn't let go of that silk portrait. And what became of that portrait later, no one knows.

His wife got nothing too. How could she when all the iron and copper had been mortgaged?

Nobody saw Tanyushka since then — like she never existed at all. Nastasya mourned her, o'course, but not too long. Tanyushka was the breadwinner, for sure, but she never felt like the girl was hers, after all.

Nastasya's sons grew up by that time. They both got married and she got to have a bunch of grandkids. The hut got all crowded then. So Nastasya didn't have a calm minute to herself, looking after them all.

There was one bachelor guy, you know. He would come and wait under Nastasya's windows. And he would stay there and wait — maybe Tanyushka would show. But she never did. Later he married someone, like all others. But they all remembered Tanyushka once in a while "Such a girl we had in the village! No equal to her can be found."

One little thing people started talking about, though. Since then the Lady of the Copper Mountain sometimes showed as a double: two lizards or two girls in the malachite dresses. People saw two instead of one.

Two Little Lizards

Our village — Polevaya — was built by the Tzar's estate, you see. There were no plants or factories here at that time, and things were hard, and lots of shady folks[12]. That's how it goes when the owner is out of sight.

So they sent soldiers to bring things to order. They even put up a village called Mountain Shield to make sure the newcomers would travel safe.

Gumeshki, you see, was becoming famous those days because lots of riches just lay about on the surface — so folks would flock around to mine stuff while they could. And, o'course, mine they did.

And then they gathered us common people, constructed a plant, even invited some Germans to manage it. But things just didn't go as well as they should've. They tried and tried, but the plant wouldn't give any profit. Mayhap the Germans didn't want to reveal their secrets — or maybe they didn't know something themselves.

Whatever the snag was, the Gumeshki mine got to be neglected by them in the end. They wanted to use a different mine, but that one was thin and poor — nothing worthwhile to be found down there. And there was no point to build a plant near it. That is how our Polevaya got in Turchaninov's hands.

---

[12] This story must take place earlier than the previous ones, judging by the fact that the copper plant described in the previous tales is about to be built when it starts. Yet, it felt like a proper place for it here because *The Two Lizards* picks up where *The Malachite Box* ended, it seems. We appear to be dealing with an anachronism since people started seeing two lizards after our heroine Tanyushka, who lived much later, disappeared from the village. Yet, the collective unconscious is dreamlike, and fairy tales are not always logical. So let's accept it for what it is, a beautiful folktale.

Barin Turchaninov[13], he used to deal in salt, trade on the Stroganovs' lands, and he had fingers in the copper business too. He had a plant, but it wasn't doing too well. That plant was not much better than our folks' handmade stuff. They burned ore in piles, then heated it till it melted, and then boiled it some more — and the owner got some profit. Turchaninov, you see, liked profits.

So, when he heard that the estate's copper plant was doing from bad to worse, he approached them and asked if he could oversee it. "We are used to the copper business," he said. "We will sort things out."

The Demidovs[14] and other plant owners — the ones who were more well-off and famous — they stayed away from it. They thought if the Germans couldn't make it there, what's the use of this plant? Only losses and waste, they thought. So Turchaninov was given this plant and Sysert, to boot — all this wealth, and for free!

Turchaninov came to stay in Polevaya and brought his own metal masters. He made a lot of promises to them, of this and that. He, the barin, knew how to get us folks to do what he wanted. He would have anyone around his pinky finger.

"Do your best, my old friends," he said. "I'll owe you till the end of my days."

Such a sweet tongue he had. He was an old hat, that one, he knew exactly what to say to spur them up. "Aren't you better than those Germans, eh?" he sang in their ear.

---

[13] Alexiy Turchaninov is a real historical figure. He was, indeed, an important plant owner. He got hold of some state-owned plants around 1759, and was known to be a successful businessman back in the day. The other plant owners mentioned in the tale were also real. However, we have no information about how much truth there is in the Tales as to their actions or words.

[14] The Stroganovs and The Demidovs were families of landowners and successful business people.

The old masters were reluctant to move from their old places, but this word about the Germans ticked them off. They didn't want to make like they were not as good as the German masters. Those Germans, you know, they would look down on our folks — like they didn't even see them as equals.

So the old ones took offense, o'course. They looked around the plant and saw that it was well-organized, with all the proper equipment, better than the first Turchaninov's plant. Sure, the Tzar's estate built it, you know.

Then they went to see Gumeshki, looked around the ore there and said "What fools worked here, eh? This ore here will easily yield good metal, half-and-half. Provided we have enough salt that is, like we are accustomed to."

They, you see, had a secret. They added salt when they melted ore. That was their hope here. Turchaninov made sure his masters could do the job and fired those Germans saying "We don't need your services no more."

What could the Germans do? They got to packing. Some set for home, some for other Russian plants. But they couldn't stop wondering how our common folks would manage a plant like this. So they talked to a couple of newcomers who were employed at the plant.

They said "Look closely, these masters must have some sneaky secret. What do they hope for with ore like this? And, if you find something out, let us know; we'll pay you well."

But one of those new guys refused to spy. He told our masters what was up. And the master said to Turchaninov "You'd better hire our guys only to work in our plant. You see how things are. If we hire a stranger, mayhap he is a spy for those Germans. You profit from our secret too, eh?"

Turchaninov agreed to that, o'course, with a sly grin, and thought to himself *"I will profit even more than y'all think, huh!"*

Those days, ya see, the Demidovs and other plant owners around here liked to hire runaways, as well as Bashkirs, old-believers and others. Such workers were cheaper, they said, and with no one to answer for them to. You can do whatever you want with them.

But Turchaninov thought different. He thought *"So I'll hire workers like this, from here and there, but could I handle them? Mayhap not. Runaways are sly; they may plan something behind your back. Bashkirs, they are of an odd faith, and their language is not like ours here — who knows what they could get up to. I'll lure the locals from my own plant, from far away. And I'll move them here with their families. Where will they run if their families are here? Things will be calm and quiet like this, and, if they rebel, I'll show them a tight fist. So we'll see who makes a bigger profit. As for runaways or bashkirs, they should be kept well away from the plant."*

And, you see, that's how it has turned out. Every man from our plant lived by the one law and was of the one faith. When I visited Taghil, you know, I saw those of many different faiths, but for us it would be unheard of to have a person of a different faith around here. And we were all Slavs here, except maybe the overseers. Lots of thought was put in it, eh?

So, when the old smelting masters told Turchaninov who they would like to have as workers, he was real keen on that. He even said to them "Thank y'all, old sons, for your wise advice. I'll remember you as long as I live. I'll do as you say — close our own plant and move all those folks to this one. And you look out for the most reliable ones, I'll buy them out or rent them from their barins. Please do your best to find some good ones, and I'll ..."

And he made more high promises. Promises came easy with him. He poured the masters wine, treated them to some delicious food and sat down to feast with them, singing songs and dancing. He made up to those old masters properly, you see.

When they came back home, they praised and praised the new spot and the barin. "Lots of space there is, the soil is rich, the copper is fine, and one who moves there will make good money for sure. And the owner is our guy; he drinks and parties with us like with equals. We can live under one like him."

And then Turchaninov's people arrived, making sure the locals would agree to move. In the end, they found more than enough volunteers for the plant and for other necessary works as well. Some got taken out for rent, others were bought out. We were still bonded in those days, you see. People were sold and bought like cattle.

So, with no delay, all those folks and their families were moved to the new place — our Polevaya village. That same summer it was done. And there was no way back, o'course. Even the ones who were free and hired couldn't go back; they were in such debt for the move, they wouldn't pay it out till the day they died. Also, who would run away from their family? Blood is blood, Turchaninov had thought of everything. All those folks were as good as chained to the new place.

There was only one guy left from the old workers at the plant, the one who told our masters about the Germans' dirty plan.

Turchaninov wanted to send him into the mountain like the others, but one master stopped him. "Why would you do that? He was of good use to us, this one. We need to keep him at hand; he is smart."

And then he asked the guy "What did you do when the Germans were here?"

And the guy said "I was an *erzmuhler*."

"What kind of job is that?" they asked. And he said "That's to walk around the grinder and make sure the ore is ground evenly and sieve it."

"That's not much of a job, to work the sieve," they said. "Do you know what they used to melt ore with?"

"Nay," he said. "They didn't let us anywhere close. They had a man of their own. We only brought whatever he told us. So I kenned a li'l from what he asked for. I really wanted to know the business. I sometimes sneaked in to look at what the copper cleaner did too. But they never let us close to the smelting pots."

The master listened to that and decided "I'll take you on as my apprentice. I'll teach you properly, and you'll give me some tips about what you gleaned from the Germans, eh?"

That is how this guy — Andrukha was his name — ended up working at the furnaces. He was a quick study and soon was as good as the old master who taught him.

***

Two years passed. The plant was much different from when the Germans were here. Much more copper was mined, and our Gumeshki became famous. Rumors about our mines walked the earth. More people came to stay, and all from the same places where Turchaninov's old plant used to be.

Lots of folks worked at the furnaces, and even more in the mountain. Turchaninov's greed grew too; more and more money he wanted. So, no matter how many people came, he found work for them all. He got richer and richer, you know.

Even the Stroganovs were green with envy. They sent a petition to the Tzar's department saying that the Gumeshki mine was on their actual land and shouldn't have been passed to Turchaninov. The mine should be taken from him and given to them, the Stroganovs, they said.

But Turchaninov was in power back then. He kept company with princes and senators as equals. The Stroganovs lost. O'course they did, when the barin had all that wealth.

But us, common folks, we didn't have it easy. And the old smelting masters were bitter, for he cheated them out of what had been promised.

At first, he walked around them on tiptoes, you see, when the business was just starting. "A little patience, old sons. Moscow wasn't built in one day, eh? Let's get the plant running smoothly, and then you'll take a breather."

But what breather? The longer the plant ran, the harder things became. The miners had it worst of all. People were flogged to death, and the furnace overseers were mad dogs. They would deal hard blows even to the best of masters and hiss "So what if you showed your copper secret? Now we can do all the smelting without you. We'll tell on you to the barin, you'll know how hard life can be."

Turchaninov was called Barin then, you know — just Barin; no other name was needed. He stopped showing up at the plant by then. He was too busy, you see, all that money needed counting, eh?

So the old masters who had talked our folks into moving here decided "We need to go see him. He is a barin, o'course, but he is our guy, eh? He knows what's right and what's wrong. He must remember how we sat at one table and drank out of one jar. We'll tell him everything straight."

So they went, all of them, but weren't allowed to see the barin. "Barin," they were told, "just had his coffee and turned in for a nap. You people go back to your plant and work as you should."

Our guys made some noise at first. "What nap?" they grumbled. "It's midday, why would he be taking a nap? Wake him up, you, his people have come to see him."

And the barin finally showed. He had had enough sleep, it looked like. And there were some armed guards with him. Andrukha, the apprentice, he was shouting louder than others, Barin this and Barin that. He even told the barin "Do you remember our salt? Where would you be without it?"

(the salt to smelt copper with, ya ken)

"Aye," says the barin. "O'course I do. Take this one, flog him and salt him up proper. So he remembers too."

They took others, o'course, the ones that the barin pointed to. But he was sly as a fox, people say. He gave orders so that they'd take out the rebels and the chatty ones.

The barin had not set foot in the plant for a while now, but he had his spies who told him who said what. So they flogged the loud ones, and the quiet ones were left alone. He just threatened those. "Watch close, you. You'll get the same treat if you don't work as you should."

The other ones got all scared, started working double and looked over their shoulder so that the spies wouldn't tell on them too. But you see, they didn't have enough people to work because of all that, and o'course they started to have losses in their business.

They began looking for the old masters and putting them to work at the furnaces again. And the one who had taught our Andrukha — he was not among the living any more. They had flogged him to death, you know.

So Andrukha was taken in his stead. He turned out to be a good smelting master, to begin with. His shifts had the best results. Turchaninov's people noted that and got to making jokes at his expense. They called him Salted, but he didn't take offense. He even joked back at them. "Salted meat lasts longer, huh?"

He got trusted like that, you see, and, just when they thought nothing bad of him, froze two furnaces at once — he had left slag[15] in there. And nothing could be done about that. Smart he was, our Andrukha.

He was taken, o'course, and chained up in the mountain. The miners, they had heard about him a lot and tried to get him out, but it wouldn't work. There were guards next to him, and everybody had to be accounted for at all times. Couldn't be helped, that.

And if you are chained up like that, how long will you stay strong? Even the strongest ones won't last long, eh? They would feed him when they wished. As for water, sometimes they forgot to bring it at all so he had to drink whatever was down at his feet in the mine. But that water is bad for one's heart, you ken. Unhealthy it is.

He got from bad to worse like that, on a chain, for six months or maybe a year, and became all weak — just a shadow left of the guy, what mining to ask from him.

So the mine overseer says "You'll get your relief soon enough. We'll dig you a hole right here, don't you worry." He is ready to bury our guy, and Andrukha himself sees how bad he is. But he is young, and he has no death wish.

And he thinks *"They talk about the Lady of the Mountain, they say she helps us poor folks... If she was real, she would help me, no? She must have seen how I've been on a chain down here for so long. But it's all just fairytales, ain't it?"*

---

[15] slag - waste matter separated from metals during the smelting or refining of ore.

He thought this and dropped where he stood — just fell like a stone into the muddy water of the stope. The water was cold, but he felt none of that.

***

How long he lay like that, he didn't know, but he got warm all of a sudden. It's like he is lying on the grass, a gentle breeze is blowing, and the sun rays are gentle and hot like it's harvest time. So he lies like this and thinks *"My death must be near, and my last dream is about a sunny day."*

But then it got hotter and hotter — scorching, no less. He opened his eyes and didn't believe what he saw. He wasn't in the mountain no more, but lying on some grassy hill in the middle of a forest. The pines are tall as tall, the grass is short and scarce, and there are some little black stones in between — like tiles. And there is a huge stone on his right, as high as a wall, taller than those pines even!

Andrukha began to poke at himself — mayhap he was sleeping? He would touch the stone, move a blade of grass, rubbed his feet. Muddy they were, o'course, from all his time in the stope. And he saw that he wasn't dreaming, in the end — the mud on his feet and legs was real, but the chains were gone.

"Eh," he figured. *"They must have thought I was dead and took me out of the mine. And here I am, not dead, ain't I? But what shall I do now? Run away or wait and see what happens? I wonder who put me here."*

He looked around and saw that there was a jar next to the stone, and there were slices of bread on top of it. He was real glad. *"Must have been my own guys who put me here then. And they didn't think me dead — even left me some drink and bread. Mayhap they'll come to see me when it's dark. That's when I'll find out what's what."*

Andrukha ate up the bread, drank up the jar to the bottom. And a funny drink it was, he couldn't make out which kind. Not like beer or wine, but it boosted his strength like magic.

After the meal he felt even better. He liked that place so much he could just stay there forever. But then he thought *"What next? Mayhap, my own guys will come, but what if the overseer and his men find me out? I should look around, see where I am. I wish I could get into a banya[16] now — and some clothes would do nicely too."*

So he got to thinking. That's how it is, a living man will think about his living needs. He climbed on top of a stone and saw that Gumeshki and the plant were close by, and he could even see some people crawling about like ants.

Andrukha got worried even — what if someone noticed him from up where he was? He got off that stone, sat in his old place and began thinking his thoughts while a bunch of lizards ran around him.

So many they were and all different colors. But two of them were odd, not like the others. They were both green, one bigger and one smaller.

And so they frolicked in the sun, those lizards, hopping around in the grass as if playing. "They must like the sunshine too," he thought. Thus, he watched the lizards and didn't notice how a cloud covered the sun.

A drizzle began, and all the lizards hid at once. Only the green ones didn't go away, just kept playing tag with each other — closer and closer to where he sat. But when the rain started in earnest, they, too, found shelter underneath

---

[16] A banya is similar to a sauna, but there are hot stones there on which one is supposed to pour water so there is steam. Going to the banya was more than just a cleaning procedure. It could be an event for people to socialize and have a good time together.

a stone. One moment he saw them, and then they just vanished into thin air, it looked like. He thought it funny.

He didn't hide from the rain, though. It was warm and wasn't going to last long. Instead, he took off his rags. *"It'll wash away some of the dirt, at least,"* he figured. So he laid his rags around so that the rain would rinse them well.

When the rain stopped, the lizards came back, dashing back and forth, dry and happy. And Andrukha, he was getting cold. The evening was drawing near, and the sun wasn't as warm anymore. He wondered about those lizards. *"I wish I could do the same. Find a stone to hide under — and here is your home."*

He leaned against that large stone that he had climbed before to look about from. He didn't really put his full weight on it, but the stone rocked and moved like it was some kind of a door. Andrukha jumped away, and the stone set back in its original place.

"What a strange stone," he thought. *"So huge, and so unstable. I could have been caught under it."*

But he came closer again, walked around to see it better. With no gaps or holes in sight, it looked like the stone was sitting fast in the ground. He tried to move it from the left and from the right, but the stone felt like it was part of a large rock and wouldn't budge an inch.

"Perhaps I was just lightheaded. I was seeing things." Andrukha thought and sat back where he was before.

Those two green lizards came back too, running around him. One touched the stone with her head — where Andrukha had leaned on it in the first place — and the stone rocked lightly. There appeared a gap along the whole long side of it. The lizard snuck inside, and the gap vanished. The other lizard ran to the opposite side of the stone and hid there, like guarding the exit. But meanwhile it eyed Andrukha, as if saying *"My friend is going to come back soon. I'll wait."*

He waited too. The other side of the stone developed an identical gap, and, as the gap grew, the first lizard showed its little head to look around as if to see where the other one was. And the second lizard was still, like it wasn't a moving-living creature at all.

So the first one sprung out, and the other one jumped on its back — gotcha! — like they played a game and it won. And then they both ran somewhere and were nowhere to be seen. It was like they showed Andrukha where to enter that stone, and where to exit.

He looked over the stone once again. It looked whole, with no gaps or imperfections — not even a trace of where to get in. *"Let's try one more time,"* he decided. *"Won't hurt, eh?"*

So he leaned on the stone where he did before, and the stone almost rolled on top of him. But Andrukha didn't care — he just gawked at what was below.

There was a stairway, and a proper one, like in a barin's new house. He stepped onto that stairway, and the lizards ran in front, showing him the way. He went down two more steps and was still holding on to the stone as he thought *"If I let go of it, it'll roll back and I'll be stuck in the dark here."*

So he stood, and the two lizards stopped and looked at him, waiting. Finally, Andrukha figured out *"The Lady must be testing my courage, that's what it is. They say she loves to do just that."*

And he made up his mind. He walked down some more and, when his head was at the level of the entrance gap, he let the stone go. The stone rolled back on top, but it wasn't dark. It was like a sun rose somewhere below, and it was light as day.

He saw large double doors made of stone, and there were beautiful carvings on those doors. On the right there was a simple door, small and unadorned. The lizards stood in front of it, like showing him *"That's where you want to go."*

Andrukha opened the door and saw a banya inside — a real proper banya, but everything was made of stone. There was a seat, and a bucket with a ladle and all that stuff. Only the vihta[17] was birch. And it was hot as hot inside that banya — your ears could burn.

Andrukha was real happy. He wanted to wash and dry his rugs first in front of that stone hearth. But, as soon as he took them off, they disappeared. He looked behind him and saw some new shirts and other clothes hanging in the closet — all kinds of garments: worker's, barin's, merchant's stuff.

Andrukhka didn't think long. He got onto that hot stone seat and whipped himself with that vihta as long as his heart desired. He got all warm and clean and sat down to catch his breath. He then found some working clothes — like the ones he was used to wearing — and opened the small door to get out.

The lizards waited for him at the big doors with the carvings.

He pulled on that door and stopped. What a wonder! He sees a huge room like he has never seen before. The walls in that room are all covered with fancy stone patterns, and there is a table in the middle, with all kinds of dishes and drinks.

He was hungry, o'course. He didn't think twice, just sat at the table. The food was all familiar, but the drink was strange, sort of like he drank from that jar earlier — a potent drink, but doesn't make you drunk. So he ate and

---

[17] A sauna whisk

drank till he was full, like at a wedding or some other big feast, and then bowed to the lizards. "Thank you, dear hostesses, for this treat."

And they sat on a tall bench nodding their little heads, like saying *"You are very welcome, dear guest."*

Then one of them — the smaller one — hopped off the bench and ran somewhere. Andrukha followed it. It took him to a bed and halted there — *you can rest here*, like. The bed was so well made he was afraid to touch it. But still, tired as he was, he lay down and fell asleep at once.

And the light went out.

***

Meanwhile, the mine overseer raised the alarm. He looked in on our guy in the morning — to check if he was still alive — and saw only the chain.

He got all worried and started running like a chicken with its head cut off. "Where is he? What do I do now?"

So he runs and runs round and round. Our guy is nowhere to be found, and no one to suspect who could have helped him. He fears he'll have to answer for Anrdukha himself if he tells his bosses.

He wasn't too smart, that one, but thought of a way out. He found some stones at the sides of the stope and piled them inside it. And then he went to tell his boss. "Look," the overseer said. "There must have been a stonefall overnight, he is under there, only one chain is left from the guy."

His boss, it looked like, didn't know much about anything so he believed the overseer. And that one kept on saying "There is no point in digging him out now, eh? The whole stope is weak, the ceiling could cave in. Besides, there is no good ore here anymore, and the deadman doesn't care where he lies, does he now?"

Our miners saw that the stonefall was fake, o'course, but kept quiet. They thought *"The man has had enough at last. Let him lie and have his final rest."*

So the overseer's boss said to the barin "Our Salted guy got buried under a stone fall — the one who froze our furnaces back then."

And the barin — sly as he was — used this for his benefit. "The man was punished by God himself," he said. "We need to tell the priests about this so they can preach about it to the serfs. It'll be a lesson for them not to mess with the barin."

The priests began their preaching, o'course. Everybody found out that Andrukha got buried in the stonefall down in the mine. They were sorry for him, sure. "He was a good man," they said. "Not many like him are left."

***

And our Andrukha? He just slept and slept. The bed was warm and soft to his tired body. He slept for a couple of days, then turned on the other side and fell asleep again. By and by, he had enough sleep and rest and felt well again — like he was never sick and hadn't spent all that time in the mountain.

When he finally woke up, the table was ready for him again, and the two lizards sat on the bench, looking at him with their lively eyes.

He ate and drank and then bowed to the lizards. "Thank you, my dear hostesses. And now it is time to thank the barin for his salt. I'll make him a thank-you present like no other."

One lizard — the smaller one — hopped off the bench and ran somewhere. He followed it. The lizard led him to another door. He pushed it and saw a stairway that went up all the way to the ceiling. There was a little bracket up there, like a handle. Andrukha figured out what it was for.

He got up the stairway, pulled the bracket and opened the hatch. Andrukha got out and found himself at the same hill, and he saw it was sunset at that time.

"That," he thought *"is exactly what I need. I'll go to the mine while it's dark. Mayhap I'll see some of our guys and ask around what is up around here."*

He headed in that direction, walking slowly so that nobody saw him who shouldn't have. He came close to the mine and hid behind a heather bush. There were many people around there, but he didn't know what to do. They stood in groups and he didn't recognize anyone.

It got dark as dark. Finally, one of the men was left by himself, and Andrukha recognized him. That one was a good guy, reliable if only a bit simple. They had stood at the furnace together, and the guy was sent to Gumeshki as well. Andrukha called out to him in a low voice. "Hey Mikhailo, come, come."

The guy heard Andrukha's voice and came closer but then stopped. "Who's that?" he asked.

"Come here, I say."

Mikhailo halted like he was afraid. Andrukha stuck his head out of the bush so the other guy would see him for who he was. Mikhailo gave a little cry and ran off. And, to Andrukha's bad luck, some woman from the village came by that same place. She saw Andrukha too and got to screaming for real — one's ears would hurt!

"Oh my, oh my, deadman walking, deadman!"

And Mikhailo shouted "Salted Andrukha just showed in front of me. I saw him just like he was living, behind that heather bush, right there!"

Folks started to fuss and worry. Some ran away from the mine, and the bosses were the first to run. Others said "Let's go look." And they went all together, but Andrukha didn't want to show himself in front of a crowd. Who knows what kind of people there were among them?

He hid farther away, in the forest. The folks got fearful — too dark in between the trees at night — and went all back home.

Andrukha thought up something new. He went past Gumeshki, through the woods, and found himself at the copper plant. Those who saw him there got scared, o'course. They threw their tools and ran wherever they could. The night overseer even climbed the roof so afraid he was.

By the next day, when they took him off that roof, he had lost all his wits and couldn't remember who he was. So Andrukha had the plant all to himself, and he froze all the furnaces like the time before.

The barin, he heard about the deadman walking, you see. He ordered the priests to go to the plant — but they were nowhere to be found somehow. Then the barin locked his house and said to open the door to nobody.

Andrukha saw that nothing more was to be done and went back to the stone room inside the mountain. But he thought *"You wait! I'll think of something to help you remember your salt!"*

The day after there was a lot of fuss about the plant. The furnaces were all frozen, with slag inside them. That stuff is no joke, for sure. The barin was in actual tears.

There was a lot of bustle around the Gumeshki mine as well. He, the barin, told them to dig out our guy from under the stone pile and give him to the priests so that they could bury him properly and he wouldn't walk the earth anymore.

They moved away the stones in Andrukha's stope, but there was no dead body underneath. They only found the chain, and it was undamaged — like nobody filed it off or anything.

By and by, they asked for the overseer. He tried to weasel out of it and blame the workers, but had to confess in the end. So the barin was told what had happened, and everything changed at once! The barin got real cross and bellowed "So he is alive, is he! Catch him you stupid fools!"

And he sent his guards to search the forest.

***

Andrukha didn't know that and went outside in the evening again. The stone palace was beautiful, for sure, but he felt better out on that hill and in that grass. He sat by the stone and thought about how to go meet his friends. He had a girl too, you know. *"She must be thinking I am dead. I wonder if she cried at all about me."*

And, just his luck, some village women were walking by. Mayhap they were coming home from some haymaking or had been picking some late berries. Lots of people there are out and about in the summer, eh? So they walked in the forest, close to that hill where he was. First Anrukha heard their singing and then their chatter.

One of them said "I wonder what Tasyutka thinks. She must have heard her Andrukha is alive and well." And the other said "Sure, alive he is — how else would he've froze all the ovens?"

"So what about Tasyutka? Did she go look for him?"

"Such a fool," another one said. "I told her yesterday that he is alright, but she believes her witch of a grandmother. Tasyutka, she is much afraid that Andrukha will come to her window at night — and she bawls and bawls like the cow she is."

"So daft. She does not deserve a guy like him. If he was mine, I wouldn't be scared of him even if he was dead."

Andrukha listened to this and got real curious who was calling his Tasyutka such names. And he also thought *"Mayhap I can pass a message through them to her?"*

He went in the direction of those women's voices. He knew those girls but saw that he couldn't show up in front of them. Lots of people walked with them, and kiddies too. How would he, "the deadman", show himself?

Andrukha watched them for a while but didn't say anything. He just turned back and sat in his old place. Sad and bitter he was. And, while he was gone, some Barin's dog must have seen him and told on him. The hill got surrounded by the barin's guards. Real glad they were. The main one shouted "Take him!"

Andrukha saw them running to get him from all sides. He pushed the stone and dived down. The barin's guards ran to that spot — and there was nobody there.

Where is he, they think? So they push and pull the stone. They puff and pant, but the stone won't budge. So they think in fear *"He must be dead indeed, the way he went down into the ground."*

They ran to tell the barin what they saw. He shook with fright when he heard the news. "I need to go to Sysert," he said. "There is some urgent business I need to attend to. You catch him without me. And, if you don't, you'll get no mercy from me!"

So he threatened them, jumped on the horse and galloped off. The servants and guards didn't know what to do. They decided to go back to the hill and wait.

***

Meanwhile, Andrukha was there, under the stone. He, too, didn't know what to do. He wasn't one to sit still, but he couldn't come out neither.

"I'll wait for the nightfall," he thought. *"I'll try my luck then. Mayhap I'll sneak out when it's dark, and I'll figure what to do next afterwards."*

So he decided to leave and wanted to take some food with him, but the lizards were nowhere to be seen. He felt bad taking their food without them seeing — like stealing.

"Eh," he thought. *"I'll do without. If I live, I'll find bread somehow."*

He looked around that stone palace room. Pretty it was, and everything was in its place. And he said "I thank this dwelling and will now leave for another one."

That is when the Lady showed herself to him in her proper shape. Our guy stood speechless so beautiful she was!

And she told him "You can't go out the same way anymore. You'll have to go elsewhere now. And don't think about food. You'll get enough when you want; you deserve this. The tunnel will let you out where you want it to. Go through that door but don't look back. Remember, don't look behind you. Got it?"

"I won't," he answered. "Thank thee for all your kindness, Lady." He bowed to her deeply, turned and saw the exact same woman at the other door — but it's like she was ever prettier than the first one.

He forgot himself, looked back — what of the first one? And the Lady grins at him as she shakes her head. "Have you forgotten what I told ya?"

"Yes," he says. "I've lost my mind from all this beauty."

"Huh," she says. "And they call him Salty! Such a proper guy he is in all respects, but cannot sort out which girl is which. What shall I do with you?"

"Do what you will," he says.

"Oh, well, I'll forgive you this once. But don't turn around again. You'll call bad luck on your head."

Andrukha went to the door, and the other one opened it for him. There was a tunnel behind it, light as day, and he couldn't see the end of it.

Did he turn around again? I don't know that. My old ones didn't say, and neither did they know where that tunnel led him out. Nobody saw him around here ever since, but folks remembered about him.

Turchaninov got a real salty present from him, huh?

And the other ones — Turchaninov's guards — they waited around that stone for a long time, day and night. Our folks went to look-see those fools. But then they probably got tired of all that waiting. They wanted to blow that stone up with powder. Our miner guys were ordered to break up that whole hill.

And the barin — he came to his senses by then and wasn't afraid no more — he stomped his feet and shouted at them. "You fools!" he screamed. "You had nothing better to do than to guard an empty stone while Gumeshki lost all profits. And the bailiff's ass got burned, to boot. What the heck are y'all good for?"

The Malachite Necklace

And you'll ask me, how come there were two of them, eh? That, my dear one, is a thing people have wondered about, o'course.

And another thing. My old 'uns told me no one knows what became of Andrukha, but I ken he came out of there alright. Otherwise, how would folks know that the Lady helped him? He must've told someone about it, I reckon.

Anyhow, here is what I've heard about the other girl under the mountain.

Do you remember Danilo, the Stone Master? He had a bunch of kiddies with his Katya, and all lads. And they all took after their father in the malachite craft. That is how things were done back then, you know. The little ones started to help the big ones when they could still walk under a table.

Alexiy was the oldest, and a fine malachite carver. He took after his father, that one, both in his looks and his love for the craft. Whatever trifle he had to carve, he put his soul in it — even if the barins ordered it just to show off in front of other rich folks. He would make buckles that looked like real beetles; he would work out a butterfly brooch that seemed about to take flight; and his snake bracelets appeared to move around the arm they were put on — pretty and lifelike, people say.

Danilo never told him about his time as the Lady's apprentice, how could he? But there were rumors from before the time he disappeared. In a village people talk, you know. "Ya daddy's work is magic," some old masters told him. "He says he went to Kolyvan to study, but we know nobody over there with such technique. He must've stayed with the Lady."

"Daddy," Alexiy would ask. "Did you really see the Lady's palace?" But Danilo would only shake his fair head. "Old wives' tales! Don't listen to those who know nothing about anything, eh? We love the stone, and it loves us back, that's why our tricks come out so pretty."

He would pat the lad on the shoulder and say "Look at your work. Your snakes and lizards are fine, and we get a good coin for them, do we not?" And then he would get lost in thought and become dreamy-eyed. He would get all quiet and gloomy then.

Alexiy took after Danilo in other ways. "My snakes and lizards," he would say. "They are pretty, for sure. But not like a living-breathing thing... The real ones are quicksilver, the way they move. Mine are nothing but toys for the fat wallets who like flashy trinkets."

Meanwhile, the old Turchaninov had died and his son inherited the plant and the land around it. Lots of hustle and bustle there was in Polevaya around that time; a new bailiff had come and gone. And the young barin — they say he lost his wits over a village girl he met here, in our land. Tanyushka she was called, and people say she was as beautiful as the Lady herself. No wonder all our guys — and the barin too — had been head over heels about her.

Only that girl, she went to Aint-Peterburg and never returned. They say something strange happened there — like she vanished into thin air, and that's why the young barin got so distraught.

Whatever happened, nobody saw her ever since, and the barin took to the bottle. Strange times there were for the plant workers, but the malachite carvers still did alright. There were lots of orders from other lands because our mountains are special, you see. People say the Lady of the Copper Mountain is really fond of her stones and takes a liking to ones who appreciate their beauty. Our masters have been touched by her, they say.

Anyway, the young barin's auntie came for a visit around that time. Barin Turchaninov was away, but she came to stay. Mayhap she hoped to save the copper business he had given up on; or maybe she thought she would get some other profit, who knows.

She had heard of Katya and Danilo's workshop, o'course. Danilo was called the Stone Master for a good reason, and his skills were known all around our big country. So she thought of some fancy thing she wanted made and came to the workshop.

Danilo was sick on that day; malachite looks pretty but does ugly things if you breathe it in for days on end. His wife Katya came out to greet her. "Good day," she nodded to the barinya. "What brings you here, your highness?"

The barinya told her what she wanted. She wished to have a bracelet that looked like a little snake, made out of malachite and finished with golden foil. She even had a drawing from Aint-Petersburg. She said some French Dutchess had one like this, and she wanted one too.

Katya said that Danilo was unwell but she, Katya, could make it for her. The barinya only gawked at her — a woman, carving malachite? No.

At that time Alexiy came in, and she couldn't but stare. He was as handsome as his father used to be, fresh-cheeked and tall, with a head full of fair curls. "Can *he* do it?" the barinya said.

Alexiy, he had too much on his plate already — working his and Danilo's orders — but she was the barinya. Her family owned the land they lived on. He said yes, o'course, thinking *"Pops has some trifle like that in his workshop; maybe I can re-work it. But we don't have gold, doesn't she know that? Stone is free to come by, but golden foil..."*

And the barinya, as if reading his thoughts, said "I have a golden chain I don't like. Come by the house tonight, and I'll give it to you. You can use that for the finish."

Katya only shook her head when the barinya left. They had a lot of orders, and that was good, but the barin and his pals and such would mess up other orders' timing. Besides, Danilo was sick, and she worried about him. People here didn't live long, you see. Some worked with stone like Katya and her man, others, even worse, would spend days inside the mountain, mining copper, mainly, and that same malachite. Danilo's cheeks were showing green already, and his blond hair looked like old copper too.

Evening came, and Alexiy showed up at the barin's house, as instructed. A servant girl led him into the barinya's quarters and offered him some real tea. He knew what tea was, o'course, but what they had at home was usually made of herbs. The tea tasted bitter to him as he waited for the barinya.

They had agreed that the bracelet would be ready in four days, but the barinya sent for Alexiy on the night of the second day. "Come over for a cup of tea and treats. As a little thank-yee for your work."

She got a liking for the guy, people said. It wasn't rare that a barin would take a liking for one of us, simple folks, and bonded ones had no choice, girl or boy. But a barinya going for a villager, that was unheard of, and she was in Katya's years!

Anyhow, Alexiy told her servant he couldn't come because he had an urgent order from our priest — a jade bowl for the church — and it had to be done by the morning. There was a church holiday coming up, you see. Alexiy sent his apologies with the barinya's man and said he would bring the bracelet to her house when it was ready.

The day after she sent the servant again, to tell Alexiy that their due for the land had to go up. The copper plant was not bringing profit, and the barin had to make up for it — that's what people heard her say.

With a heavy heart, Alexiy asked one of the kiddies to take the bowl to the priest and got to work on the gold finish for the barinya's new bracelet.

***

Once he was done with her order and the ones he would get paid for, Alexiy went for a walk. The sun was still up, but not high at all. He roamed around the forest for a while till he found himself at a cliff. He was at an old quarry that had got flooded and became a lake. The place was beautiful, with jagged rocks and tall pines all around. Its granite walls caught the last rays of the sun and seemed golden.

"Huh," he thought. "*They don't appreciate this grey stone much, the rich ones, but why? True, it isn't as pretty as marble, but it is as strong. They could build bridges out of this stone - or houses! Plenty of it all around here. But they want their palaces done in marble or malachite, eh! Such a waste of rare stone!*"

So he sat, enjoying the view of the quarry and the mountain behind it, and there were little beasts out and about. A swallow flew past, a sparrow sat on a low branch and tilted its head at him. A lizard ran by — and halted when it saw him, like it was made of stone. He chuckled at it. "We make things out of stone, wanting them to look like you and here *you* are."

The lizard was an unusual shade of green, with lighter and darker stripes and a black spine. "Like malachite," he thought. He blinked — and it was gone, that lizard. Alexiy looked around. The light was fading so he headed home.

When he came to see the barinya on the fourth day, she didn't offer him any treats but immediately donned the bracelet. "It looks so lifelike," she sighed — as if she'd ever seen live lizards with specks of gold on their backs.

The young stone master bowed and was ready to leave, but she stopped him.

"I have heard the tales old folks tell here, about the Lady of the Copper Mountain. Is there any truth to them?" Alexiy didn't know what to say. The Lady was a mountain spirit, but their village priest told them it was a sin to believe in any except God and the angels. And here she is, asking him. If he says the Lady of the Mountain is but make-believe, she — the Lady — could take offense, you see. If he tells the barinya what he really thinks, that's heresy, eh? You can get flogged for this or worse!

"I have never seen her, your highness, and don't know anyone who has," he finally said. "And our priest says it's all nothing but old wives' tales."

The barinya looked at him and smiled. "Oh well, fairy tales or not, my new cook says people have been seeing two of them instead of one, so here is my next order for you."

Now she wanted a necklace that would look like two lizards, with their heads at the front, like they were whispering to each other, and their tails would make a clasp at the back of the neck. Alexiy would first draw the design for her and bring it to the barin's house, o'course.

The barinya waved him off, and Alexiy got to thinking how to go about that necklace and which malachite would be better for it. He decided to ask his father what he thought.

Danilo perked up when he heard what Alexiy's task was. Together, they thought of a way to make the lizards seem like they were moving on the wearer's neck. They drew a picture for the barinya, and Danilo said "Go to Snakes Mountain, mayhap you'll find the pattern you need over there."

Alexiy had heard about Snakes Mountain, o'course, and he did go there on occasion, but he never saw a pattern like they wanted. But he also heard from the old 'uns that sometimes the Lady would help them find the stone they needed if she felt like it. So he went.

***

It was April then, and the grasses were still yellow, but the birds were singing and squirrels were hopping around. The road to the mountain went through a pine forest. Few folks would use it — too early for meadow work or berry picking. He headed there after he was done with work for the day so the sun was pretty low.

The road was lonely but what would a sturdy guy like him worry about? The wolves left these parts alone — rocks don't make good pasture so no cows or sheep, eh? And he wasn't afraid of people either. What would they want with him, poor as he was? He was a good master and he made some, for sure, but there were six little ones to feed, and he didn't care much for new clothes and other nonsense.

By and by, he climbed to the top of Snakes Mountain. It wasn't much of a mountain no more, though; more like a hill. He had looked here and there but couldn't find the stone he wanted. So he decided to take a break before going home.

And, as he looked around, he spotted the quarry from the other day, not too far below. With its rocky shores, it looked like a jade pendant in a golden frame to his jeweler's eye.

Suddenly he saw a figure on the edge of the quarry's cliff. The figure stood still for a bit and then dropped into the water.

Alexiy rushed to help. It was foolish to dive like this. One never knows how deep the water may be in a quarry, or where the rocks are underneath.

By the time he arrived at the spot, though, the person appeared at the shallow side, close to where he was about to dive in himself. He saw a girl that didn't have a thread on. She chuckled as she came closer.

Alexiy didn't know where to look as she greeted him so he turned away.

"You can look now, don't be shy," she said, and, when he looked up, she was fully clothed already. Her dress seemed to be made of malachite — with the exact pattern he wanted for the barinya's necklace.

"I thought you needed help," he mumbled.

She grinned back. "But it's you who needs helping, no?"

He just stared at her and didn't know what to say for the girl was beautiful, dress or no dress. She had jet black hair and eyes like emerald fire.

"Mind your manners, young man," she said. "You can't just oggle a girl like that." But she smiled as she said that, and her voice was warm and friendly. "So, why are you here?"

He explained why he came to the mountain and pointed to her dress. "Are you the Lady?" He finally dared to ask.

"It depends." She grinned again. "Never mind that for now. I will give you the stone you want if you promise to make a necklace for me first. There will be enough stone for two."

"Your beauty is such that you don't need any jewels but I will be happy to make it for you."

"Go there," she pointed to the left of where he arrived from. You'll find what you need on that side of the mountain. But you'd better keep your word, Alexiy, Danilo's son."

He looked where she showed and, when he turned to thank her, she was gone. Like a ghost — but she was not a ghost, she was a girl, and Alexiy's heart was beating fast.

Alexiy did as she said and found the stone he had been looking for. He used his trusty pick axe to free it - and it was easy, like that stone had been waiting to be found.

***

By and by, he came back home and showed it to his father. Danilo listened to the story and only nodded his head.

The day after Alexiy went to see the barinya. She oohed and aahed when she saw that design, so pretty it was. "I want it done next week," she said. "I don't care if this is the only thing you will work on but finish it by Saint Mary's Day."

Alexiy said he could not do it in seven days, no way. *After all, he promised to make one for the green-eyed girl first*, he thought. A fortnight, he said, no earlier.

The barinya had to agree. "Alright," she said. "I will wear it for the Easter service then. But you, my dear friend, I want to see before that. Come tomorrow night, I will give you a proper meal to put some meat on your bones. And mayhap some sweet treat to polish things up," she winked. "You are good at that, polishing, I mean, eh?"

He only blinked at her so stunned he was. But she was the barinya, eh? He said he would come. *"I'll eat her food and drink her drink,"* he thought. *"After all, I am working this order of hers for free, ain't I?"*

Alexiy returned home and got to his carving machine at once. He knew he had to make two of those necklaces in the time he had bargained for, and no easy task it was. He wanted the lizards to look like they were playing or telling each other some secret things. And the malachite he found was perfect for that; the stripes and patterns were long and winding in all the right places.

Danilo became very ill at that time; he would cough and wheeze all night. Alexiy heard, and his heart ached.

The evening after, our guy had to go see the barinya, as promised. A festive table was waiting for him in the barinya's sitting room, with all kinds of food: pirozhki with cabbage and meat, vatrushki, a long dish with a huge sturgeon baked whole in the middle of the table and other such luxuries. More food than his whole family would see in a month, it looked like.

The barinya was all smiles, and dressed funny. She had a silky robe on, red with yellow and gold dragons across her back. Golden snakes were embroidered along the hem of this strange dress.

Alexiy thought to himself *"Such an odd pattern, I could use it somewhere — in a brooch or a collar maybe."* She had put his snake bracelet on her wrist, he saw.

"Call me Marie," she said. "We are going to sit and eat at one table after all."

Alexiy sat down and noticed there were too many forks and spoons at his plate. A servant poured him soup — Dashka, a young girl from his own village. She pointed with a glance which spoon he should use.

After that everything was foggy. The barinya chatted about this and that, France and Germany, and refilled his glass with dark red wine. She told him that the wine was from Bourgonia and very old; it was made thirty years ago. He wondered why rich folks would let drinks sit for so long and wouldn't the wine go bad after all this time. But the wine was alright, and stronger than the beer he was used to, so he soon felt tipsy.

Finally, when the dinner was over, the barinya took him by the hand and led him somewhere dark. This is when he came to his senses. He mumbled that was unwell and ran out of the house.

***

He did feel sick. He had drunk too much of that old wine and ate too much.

He had planned to go back to work but figured he wasn't sharp enough to carve. He thought he would walk it off, and, somehow, he found himself at that same quarry where he had met the malachite girl. It was dark, but the moon was full, and there were stars all over the sky.

He sat on a stone, at the shallow end of the lake, and glum thoughts were on his mind. He knew, o'course, what the barinya wanted, but he was not that kind of guy. He wouldn't go with girls from the village — even if there were many who wanted him to. He waited for the one he would marry, and didn't look for fun.

By and by, he heard a splash and saw the girl again. She was sitting on another stone, her bare feet in the water.

"Good evening, Lady," he said. "Good to see you again."

She only chuckled but then said "Call me Tatiana. Why are you so glum, Alexiy?"

And he told her about the necklace, and the barinya, and the tax she raised on their land when he wouldn't come, and Danilo's illness, and his little brothers. He didn't know why but he wanted to tell this girl everything, and he was not one to complain.

She frowned and asked "Why don't you go with her, eh? Is she that old and ugly?"

"I don't want her," he said. "It's you I want."

She got all quiet and looked at him for a long time.

"Go home, Alexiy," she finally said. "Everything will work out just fine for you and yours, and the barinya will get what's owed to her. Just remember to bring me my necklace on Good Friday."

He went home and decided to talk to Danilo. To his surprise, the old man looked better and was at the workshop before sunrise. Alexiy told his father about the malachite girl and his promise.

Danilo didn't ask any questions — just nodded. Lots of work they were, these necklaces, but they could still finish them if they worked together.

So they agreed that the father will work on the necklace for the barinya, and the son will carve Tatiana's. They talked some more, and together they figured out how to go about the tricky design they'd thought of.

After that they both got to carving, and Alexiy's necklace was ready by Friday morning. Danilo started later, but it was easier for him because he already had Alexiy's piece to model his by. All good and well, the barinya's piece would be ready for Easter Sunday like she ordered.

***

That day — around noon that was — the barinya herself showed up at their hut. She was all dressed up and smelled like too many flowers. She asked for Alexiy, and Katya said he was busy carving. She wanted to holler for him, but the barinya pushed her aside and headed for the workshop. Alexiy was working on another order, and the necklace he had made was lying on a small side table, next to him.

"Goodday," she greeted him coldly. "I see my order is ready." And she snatched the necklace off the table. He told her it was not finished yet. *It was, o'course, but that one was promised to the malachite girl.* But the barinya wouldn't listen — she put it in her purse, turned on her heels and was gone.

Alexiy was without words and didn't know what to do. Tatiana told him she was not the Lady, but she was not a simple village girl either. She was some magical being, and he had promised her that necklace. "*Who knows what she will do when she finds out the barinya took it?*" he thought.

Katya, his mum, saw how distraught he was. In the end, Alexiy told her the truth, about how he met the malachite girl and she helped him find the right stone. And how he promised to make the first necklace for her.

Katya raised her brow and said "So the stories people tell are true, eh? I have heard of Tanyuska from the copper plant village. But I thought the girl just ran away from our barin back then. He is dim, that one, and lustful. Some said that Tanyushka was the Lady's adopted daughter, though. That's whom you met, huh?"

Alexiy had not heard those stories. He was a man, and they don't talk much, ya know. But women, they chat about everything in their village and other ones close by as well.

Anyhow, Katya thought a bit and then said "I have met the Lady once, don't ask me how and when. I promised not to tell. She is not evil; she can be reasoned with. Go talk to Tatiana. Mayhap she'll forgive you and take the necklace that Danilo is making. After all, he is probably a better master than you are."

So, when evening came, Alexiy went to the quarry again. He wanted to see Tatiana but feared what she would say. He went by Snakes Mountain as was his usual way and stopped to admire the view at the top. He noticed there were lots of lizards by the stone where he once sat, but they all ran away as soon as he approached.

Only one remained which looked like the one he had seen earlier, but who knows — lizards are lizards, mayhap it was the same one, mayhap another. He had turned his back to the stone and was about to head for the quarry when he heard a rustle.

He looked back and saw a woman. She looked like his Tatiana but she was not. And beautiful she was, with her long dark braid and her large green eyes.

"*That*'s the Lady," he thought to himself.

"So you must be Alexiy, Tatiana's new friend," the Lady said smiling, but the smile wasn't kind or warm.

He bowed to her. "Goy, Lady, I am indeed."

"What do you want with my daughter?" she asked coldly.

Alexiy was afraid; still, he said what was in his heart. "I want to take her for my wife — if she is willing and you let her."

The Lady frowned but told him "Go ask her yourself; I'll let her if she'll have you; she is human, after all." And she pointed to the quarry. "Go, before I change my mind, and don't look back."

He bowed again and went to the quarry, wondering "They are so alike, these two. How come one is human and one is stone? Such magic..."

When he reached the quarry, there was no one to be seen. He stayed at his usual spot by then — the shallow beach — and waited. He waited a long time and thought to play his oat[18]. His father had been real good at it and taught him when he was little. But Danilo didn't play much anymore; his lungs wouldn't let him. And Alexiy didn't play because he had too much work and no idle minute. Still, he would bring the oat with him everywhere he went — for good luck.

---

[18] a shepherd's flute (archaic)

***

So he looked at the full moon and the stars and played some tune he didn't even know he knew.

After a while he heard a splash and saw the girl. She sat on the same stone as before, rocking her bare feet, and listened to his music. And she was sad as sad. He felt so happy to see her he rushed to her without a second thought. She jumped to her feet and away, quick as a cat.

"What is it you want with me?" she asked.

He bowed to her deeply, like she was the Lady herself. "Good eve', Tatiana," he said. "I come to ask for your forgiveness."

"What is there to forgive?" she frowned. "That you talked to the Lady without my will?"

"No, not that." He shook his head. "I do not regret what I said to her. This should be done in the proper way, asking the parent before the bride."

"Don't you wish to know what I'll say to that?" she said.

"Aye, more than anything! Will you be my wife?"

She said nothing, just tilted her head in thought.

"We'll see," she said after some time. "What about my bride's gift? You promised to bring my necklace today."

Alexiy was ashamed but told her everything that happened truthfully. "Do what you will with me," he bowed his head.

She just stood there for a while, and, when he looked up, he saw she was smiling.

"Don't you worry, my dear friend Alexiy," she said mildly. "I am not cross with you. I have told you things will work out for you, and they will. My necklace will take care of itself. As for the one that your father is making, ask him to bring it to Snakes Mountain when it's done. He shall leave it on the stone at the top there; he'll know which one."

"When will you give me your answer?" he asked.

"Soon. Go now. I'll see you on Sunday night."

***

That same evening, the barinya decided to try on the necklace. She took it out of her canvas bag, and it was so cold her fingers felt like ice. She fiddled with the clasp and put it around her neck. The stones had a winter chill to them but she thought *"It'll warm up soon; jewelry always does when you wear it long enough."* And she went out to the dining room like that.

She didn't have much appetite though. She was dining alone — no other nobles around here for miles, eh? She thought of the boy who turned her down so rudely last week. *"I will make him pay for that,"* she decided. *"I'll triple their due come June, you just wait."*

The necklace, meanwhile, didn't warm to her skin. Even worse, it seemed to become tighter and tighter and weigh like it was lead, not malachite, it was made of.

She was a stubborn woman, though, that one, and she thought *"It's fine, I'll take it off when night comes. I just need a little time to get used to it; gems are always heavy and cold. Look at the Tzarina, she always wears such heavy strands of beads in her portraits. I can do this too!"*

Still, she felt sick and weak, and, when Dashka, her servant, came in to ask if she wanted cake with her tea, the barinya just sent her off. By the time she got back to her chambers, she felt so weak that she just lay on the bed, on top of the blanket. She thought *"I'll just rest a bit,"* and closed her eyes.

***

They found her around noon the morning after; her face was all blue and there were bruises around her bare neck.

The barin's guards made some noise, o'course. They grabbed Dashka and shook her till she told them the barinya had only made friends with one person in our village — Alexiy.

But she, Dashka, didn't see him that evening, and, when she locked up for the night, the barinya was surely alone. The windows in the dead woman's chambers were all locked from the inside so no chance someone could've gotten in either.

After that they arrested Alexiy, no doubt about that. They put him in a make-shift jail. But they didn't have any proof against him — and they didn't care much for the barinya, to be honest. She was not ours, you know, nobody even saw her till she came o'er three weeks before. And the guards — our village guys — were not in a hurry to flog Alexiy to death for something he prob'ly didn't do.

One of the guards was Alexiy's neighbor, Yermoshka. They used to hang out at the pond together back when they were little. Yermoshka was a kind man, and fair. He talked the other ones into letting Alexiy out — at least till the barin comes back. Where would he go, they figured? All the nearby villages belonged to our barin anyway.

So they let him out on Sunday morning — it was Easter, after all, a big holiday in our country. As Alexiy walked home, he met people who wore their best to go to church, and they wished each other a happy Easter.

"Christ has risen!" one of his neighbors said to him.

"Risen indeed!" he answered like he should. And he thought to himself *"Such a strange festival... First, they tortured their god's son, then nailed him to a cross where he died slowly and in pain. And now we celebrate that he managed to come back from the dead."*

Yet, he couldn't help but feel festive himself. He was free, after all. The barinya would not pester him no more, and he would see his malachite girl soon.

Katya was busy about the house when he arrived. Danilo was at the carving machine. He had finished the other necklace and was working on their new orders. He looked much better and had stopped coughing, mostly — such good news!

Alexiy gave his mother a big hug and saw a deep line between her brows. She knew Danilo was to take the necklace to the Lady, and she worried. Alexiy kissed her on that worry line and asked for her blessing.

"He takes after his father even in this," she thought but said nothing. She gave him her blessing. "*What will be will be,*" she thought. The Lady had given her Danilo back all these years ago, but Katya felt in her gut there would be payback one day.

"If you want to go, Alexiy, I won't stop you. We will miss you dearly, but I fear the barin will go after you for the dead barinya when he arrives. He will want a culprit for sure. So go and be safe." She hugged him tight. "Say goodbye to the little ones, but don't tell them much. They don't need to know."

***

Evening came. Danilo went to Snakes Mountain but saw no one there — just two green lizards hopping about the big stone on its top. The old man did as he was asked; he left the necklace on the stone. "Thank yee, Lady," he said. "For keeping us safe." He bowed to the stone and the lizards on it and went back home.

Meanwhile, Alexiy headed for the quarry. Nobody saw him ever since. But people say, when the moon is full, you can see some odd reflections in that quarry — like a fair guy and a girl with a dark braid stand on a rock hanging above the water, and they hold hands.

But if you look up, there is nobody on that rock.

131

About the Authors

Pavel Bazhov (27 January 1879 – 3 December 1950) was a Russian writer and publicist.

Born and raised in the Ural Mountains, Bazhov was fascinated by the complex history of the land and the tales specific to the region. He started collecting the Urals' folklore when he was about twenty years old, transcribing the myths and legends he heard from villagers and mine workers for years. At the same time, he collected documentary evidence of pre-revolutionary plant and mine operations that the Urals boasted of.

He is best known for his collection titled "The Malachite Box", published in the Soviet Union in 1939. All in all, Bazov released fifty-six folk tales, half of which revolve around the mythical creature called The Lady of the Copper Mountain and her interactions with the common folk living in the area. His collection of folktales is non-exclusive, as other Urals' tales can be traced in the oral legacy of the Ural Mountains' inhabitants. Thanks to Pavel Bazhov, at least some of these exotic, obscure stories became available to the general public.

Victoria Fé is a Russian-Canadian writer and educator, with multiple non-fiction publications under her belt. Victoria also hails from the Ural Mountains, having grown up on the folklore that Pavel Bazhhov publicized. Her lifelong passion for stories and myths has led her to the current project of translating the folk tales you have just read.

"My ultimate goal," she says "is familiarizing my contemporaries with some non-mainstream heritage of Russian culture. I find these stories enthralling because they lack many of the archetypes typical for Slavic tales — or fairy tales, in general. In fact, their structure is rather peculiar, in that they combine the reality of harsh living conditions that existed in imperial Russia with the magic of whimsical mountain spirits that are neither good nor bad, from our perspective."

Being a writer in her own right, Victoria added a new story to the collection she chose to share with her readers. "As I was doing my translation, I was rooting for the characters, and this last story just wanted to be written. Most of these tales don't get a happy ending, and I figured, we could have one, after all." At this time, Victoria Fé is working on her personal collection of short stories — soon to be released.

Manufactured by Amazon.ca
Acheson, AB